GEIST
PRELUDE

FALLON O'NEILL

This is a work of fiction. Names, characters, places, and incidents are products of the author's imagination or are used fictitiously and are not to be construed as real. Any resemblance to actual events, locations, organizations, or persons, living or dead, is entirely coincidental.

World Castle Publishing, LLC
Pensacola, Florida
Copyright © Fallon O'Neill 2018
Paperback ISBN: 9781629899961
eBook ISBN: 9781629899978
First Edition World Castle Publishing, LLC, September 24, 2018
http://www.worldcastlepublishing.com

Licensing Notes

Cover: Nix Whittaker
Editor: Maxine Bringenberg

CHAPTER ONE

As with all such stories, it began with a nightmare.

Victor Roland's eyes rolled open to a haze of fog, feeling cool tiles against his flushed cheeks. He staggered up, head aching, knees trembling—wherever he was, it was cavernous and quiet. A chill ran down his spine, and Victor propped his trench coat's collar. The tattered thing was a lone shield between him and the unknown.

Regardless, he was reminded of infernal circles and dark woods of error.

His halting footsteps echoed throughout a hallway, and the mists lifted ever so slightly, revealing a nave of oaken pews and pillars—stained glass, stone, and steel. Beyond the altar Victor saw an organ, composed of bronze pipes and copper corpses, playing a dirge. The cathedral felt hollow, as if its holiness had faded long ago.

Upon the far threshold lay a door.

Something nagged at him. Victor was here for a reason. He was searching for—something. He passed by a baptismal fountain, staring into its still water. Dirty bangs drooped over his gray eyes, brow dotted with acne, a stubbled face wearing a solemn expression.

He sighed, continuing down the nave until he saw strange lights twinkling far above. Against them, he could *see* the constellations of thoughts, even with his eyes closed. Hopes and memories, twinkling and drifting, cast about by currents of want and fear. He knew their despair, how the lost and the damned swam up the ethereal streams, only to be siphoned away into a void blacker than death; and for what?

Above the door was a chiseled placard, reading,
ANIMI FIRMITAS

As he wandered, Victor saw other lights behind the windows, dancing in tune to the dirge. But the closer he came to the door, the darker everything else became. Staring beyond, he knew fear of the unknown, as something stirred in his own rising shadow—

At once, an otherworldly shriek echoed from behind as monstrous clouds wafted from the towering aberration, swallowing all. He tried to run, but collapsed under the weight of shock, caught in this roaring flood of fog. Tossed in its currents, the miasma drained all warmth, leaving him naked in darkness. Embraced by its chill, Victor felt memories slip away. He forgot the taste of food, his mother's touch, and the days of springtime.

He was nothing now.

Out of instinct Victor raised a trembling hand, his palm somehow shining in the mists. Cobalt light seared through the roiling clouds and Victor escaped the churning tide, bolting down the nave, another roar at his back. If his escape was a happy chance or a game on the shadow's part, Victor did not know, nor did he care. He burst through the gilded doors, exhausted and panicked, wits spiraling out of control, but his memory returned.

Then all went black.

#

Victor's eyes flew open. He rose from bed with a start, muttering profanity under his breath. Noise brought him back to the Waking World, a flat blur of the modern and urban. Regardless, the nightmare did not leave him for some time. Maybe he'd forgotten his medication, or maybe he'd just slept poorly. Sighing, he clicked a button on the radio, resuming the symphonies which had stopped sometime in his sleep.

Fantasie Impromptu…Chopin…Opus No. 66…bliss….

He swallowed a couple of antidepressants and scanned his dormitory room. It was a cluttered mess, with not a visible spot of plastered wall. Everything was either a bookshelf or a painting. It all smelled like yellowed pages and washed rinds, but Victor did not mind—Mr. Carroll was all the company he needed. The rabbit nestled in a small habitat on an oaken desk covered in draft upon draft of half-written dream journals, with Victor's laptop barely visible. He often sat there, trying to formulate ideas into notes, perhaps even a brief melody.

Easier said than done….

When awake, Victor chased ideas like a determined hunter after game, always shifting mental gears, which spun a complex web of relations, from Marxist theory to *Beowulf*. To anyone else, his thought processes would be a dizzying labyrinth of dead ends and passages to nowhere. But to Victor, the journey was just as sweet as the conclusion. And in dreams, his myriad obsessions converged into a cauldron of beautiful yet morbid fantasies.

Then he noticed the time. *5:37 p.m.*

Victor had seriously overslept, and had class in less than thirty minutes. He staggered toward the closet, where he cobbled together an outfit—a striped turtleneck, black slacks, and buckled boots under his trench coat. Although tattered and wrinkled, Victor wore that like a child's security blanket. His attire was based on comfort rather than fashion.

He was a young man who would have been good looking, if not for his hygienic and social apathy. Victor liked to think that stubble attractive, but knew that was an excuse to avoid shaving. Just then, he felt something familiar in his pockets.

Oh! I forgot I had that….

He pulled out a wooden box of tattered tarot cards. Though he hardly believed in fortune telling, he always kept it close. It was an heirloom, passed down for generations on his mother's side. He was interested in the mysteries of the occult, even if he'd rather not admit it. As he caressed the worn cards, Victor felt a mysterious connection. Not to any supernatural power, but a power within—something Carl Jung would have had a field day with.

When he had finally gathered most of his wits, he grabbed his books and left the dormitory, earbuds cancelling out all with Mozart's *Symphony No. 40 in G minor.* He walked down the street, and all was right with his world.

For as Nietzsche once said, "Without music, life would be a mistake."

As the minutes dragged on, Victor wandered into the arboretum, a shortcut to campus. He passed a familiar site, a chapel of broken buttresses, all gray and mossy. Beyond its threshold lay only gloom. Victor remembered spending childhood days in its shadows, playing amongst the rubble. He removed his earbuds, reflecting on this. Over time the place had become melancholy, dilapidating as he aged like a gothic giving tree. Now it was a specter of innocence and youth. As he stared, droplets of fog tickling on his brow, Victor heard something scuttle in the undergrowth. He spun around, and saw nothing.

But he felt eyes upon him, cold and unrelenting.

It's probably nothing....

Perhaps it was anxiety running rampant again. Resuming the music, he went on his way.

Yet deep down, Victor remained unconvinced that he was alone.

#

Victor stared under his desk, reading Dante's *La Divina Comedia* for the twenty-third time at the very rear of this massive classroom, buzzing with scribbling pens and the whispers of youths. The scratchy voice of Professor Swain still reached him. She stood at the far end of the lecture hall, a wiry woman with a bowl cut, as annoying as her class was boring.

I don't care about the Pythagorean Theorem. Why can't we talk about something relevant, like the history of mathematics? It was a branch of philosophy in Ancient Greece, in the days of Plato, Aristotle, and Socrates! Pity that math became its own subject – I could probably get away with quoting The Meno otherwise. Goddamn, someone is chewing gum very loudly....

He glanced at the clock. Only fifteen minutes into the lecture. He had to endure it, just like every other day of social purgatory. Victor sighed and looked about. It was hard to be non-judgmental when surrounded by murmuring idiots who just texted and gossiped all day. That was not to say that Victor was a good student. He often paraphrased Mark Twain — schooling was getting in the way of his education, as seen through his mildly autistic eyes. This class was acceptable to despise, as no sane student could tolerate Swain for five minutes.

Thus, he began his amateur compositions. Although Victor was hardly a savant, he was somewhat skilled in mimicking his musical forefathers. It was like molding a great ball of clay, watching in awe as it took form, and as he jotted down a prelude's sketch, inspiration hailed on him like a storm. Victor felt a rush of nostalgia, bombarded by memories of an inner world, memories that took on images clear as day. He called it, "the Opera House," and it was his estate. Truly beautiful, and he almost tricked his senses into beholding its glory.

"All right, if you remember from last week…," the nasally voice rattled on.

He was interrupted, again. Swain was perhaps the most wretched family name in etymological history. Just hearing it made Victor's skin crawl. At least Ms. Moist would be alliterative. But seething would not get him a passing grade, so he tried to pay attention.

"So, who can tell me what formula we use to—?"

"Pretty annoying, isn't she?" a feminine voice whispered from behind.

He turned around—it was a wonder Victor had not seen her before. Dressed in a biker jacket and torn jeans, her raven hair was long and smooth, punctuated by a bright blue streak, matching her eyes. Victor looked away, for eye contact made him uncomfortable. After all, eyes were windows into the soul, and he preferred to keep his soul to himself.

It was a weird sensation, but exciting nonetheless.

"Reading Dante, huh?" She gave a soft smirk. "Love him."

"Err…yeah," Victor mustered a reply. "Written between 1308 and 1321, quite the epic poem, and controversial for its time."

The goth girl looked surprised. "Damn, I've only read *Inferno*."

"Interesting." He didn't know how to react—how could one love a poet without reading their magnum opus? "Have you read Milton?"

"*Paradise Lost?*" The goth girl cocked her head and pondered. "No, but I know of it."

"It's a—good read...." Good read. What was he, a guttersnipe? "Coined the term pandemonium."

"Latin for all demons," she replied. "I know that much."

He was impressed by her general knowledge of classical literature. "What is your name?"

"Beatrice, but I'm going to change it the second I get the chance."

Victor took pains to keep his jaw from dropping. "L-like—"

"Yeah," Beatrice shrugged. "Like from Dante, I guess. It's still a shitty name."

Marry me, you literary succubus....

"Err...I like it."

Damn. The conversation had run its course. He had to think of something. He'd even made a conversation chart for such an occasion. But his guile had run dry—not that it was very fluid to begin with. "So—what else do you read?"

Beatrice shrugged. "Just about anything really. Orson Scott Card, heard of him?"

Victor stifled a scoff. "You mean the homophobic zealot who wrote the Ender's series? Yes, yes, I have."

She was a little shocked. "I did not know that. You didn't like it?"

"Oh no," Victor clarified. "I love the books for what they are—a coming-of-age story involving a gifted young man in an extraordinary circumstance. As for the writer, I cannot respect a man who would have same-sex couples criminalized and who would vote for Newt Gingrich," he shuddered. "That said, *Ender's Game* was well written."

Beatrice shrugged again. "Well, if you're going to judge a writer by their actions and their work, then you should rule out

Locke, Marx, Kant, and Ayn Rand, too."

"Sorry?" Victor did not quite understand. This made him feel awkward, his brain constricted by a neurological python. "Do explain."

"Locke owned slaves, Marx was an impoverished mooch, Kant was a racist dick, and Rand lived on welfare at one point. If you're going to judge a writer by their actions then their words don't mean anything, when they clearly do. We don't think of philosophers as people: we think of what they left behind."

Victor tried to retaliate, but could not justify any comeback. He had been wrong.

"What's your name?" Beatrice asked. "Dante?"

The perceived flirt caught him off-guard as he stuttered, "V-Victor."

"Beatrice," Swain's shrill voice echoed across the lecture hall. "Are you with us?"

"Yeah." The goth girl rolled her eyes. "I'm here."

Victor took social leave, propping his coat's wrinkled collar, but his anxiety rose. The classroom was filled with gibbering, fingernails tapping the desks, and that harpy's shrieking. He could almost hear the melody playing softly in his head, just loud enough to mask that blathering. He shut his eyes, thoughts in tune with its tempo.

Beautiful....

He could see the stars again as he kept rhythm. They called it a "hallucinatory" — he equated it to meditation. But as the opus continued, he noticed something was off — it wasn't his original composition, but a variation thereof. Just as regal and epic, having the same lyrics for the most part, even pleasant if he was in the mood. But right now it was wrong, too tense and dramatic. It made him notice how the jocks, or "sportsmen," as he preferred, stared at him, no doubt whispering, "What the fuck is that retard doing now?"

Victor knew that was an insult.

He had to contain a fit of resentful muttering, while trying to force the music, the wrong music, back to its softer state. As he dove deeper into his mind, the sights of the lecture hall dimmed. But Victor dug too deep and too quickly, and beheld his sanctuary, clearer than he thought possible. And then, with a mental slip, he was lost in his head.

When all vision dimmed, and when ambiance faded, homely comforts gave way to another world. The Wall of Sleep was behind, time lost all meaning, and surrealism took hold — at first. Then a voice ran through Victor's mind, like a mantra.

Do you remember, Victor?

His eyes drifted open, beholding his inner sanctum at last. Its murals were laden with deep, blue lights, as flashing neurons. The arched dome was supported by grand, gothic pillars. The balconies and rowed seats were bare, and a desk lay in the chamber's heart, identical to the one in his apartment, resting before the stage with velvet curtains.

There he sat, listening to the narration.

Do you remember this place as it used to be? This Opera House? This cornerstone of cornerstones? Once it housed the thousand faces of your psyche, but now, it is devoid of persona, little more than a vacant realm of former imagination. Perhaps it is due to age, perhaps neglect, but wonder has long since left the wonderland. For though your memories and melodies evolve, your life is dull and gray, that of a mediocre man, that which you hold in such disdain.

Awakening is not your concern, but remedying dreams before you truly forget to live, as you will soon learn. For heed my words — darkness is coming for you, and it is a darkness of your own making. Though you cannot feel it beyond anxieties and depressions, it germinates still, and all happiness will crumble without intervention.

13

For a man who does not heed his own words, even in dreams, is foolish indeed.

With that, Victor felt the Opera House fade into the misty limbo, behind a shattered mirror of fear and regret. But dreams were just that, for as he drifted back to awakening, like a diver breaching the surface of the sea, he knew the world would still be the same: dull, gray, and sorrowful, and he questioned its merit.

"Victor!" An unwelcome voice dragged him back to reality, to be greeted by the thin frown of Swain. "Are you with us?"

"Oh, umm...y-yeah...," Victor stuttered, praying she would get back to lecturing, so he could contemplate on what had just happened.

"You look exhausted. Are you all right?"

The class giggled, but he could barely hear them over sheer dread.

"You were muttering Latin...again."

"I'm fine," he replied curtly, trying to feign eye contact, staring at her forehead—an old trick. It usually worked on these people.

"All right...." She seemed unconvinced. "Just pay closer attention."

When Ms. Swain turned her back, Victor fondled his tarot cards, trying to distract himself, until one slipped out of the smoothly worn box and landed on the floor. But as he picked it up, Victor saw the Moon Arcana—the omen of dreams and fantasy. He was trembling, as the question, "What if?" burrowed into his skull. It was a question he could not answer. Only five minutes remained of the class, but it was going to be a hard push.

He looked over his shoulder at Beatrice.

Her eyes were closed. At least he wasn't alone.

CHAPTER TWO

When class ended, Victor walked down the arboretum road back to the dormitories. The fog was thicker now, soupy and somber, obscuring the way forward. Before long, he sat down by that cathedral. He hadn't put the Moon Arcana back in the box yet, holding it close, as if trying to find some rationality behind the esoteric. Making sense of this was impossible. He slipped the card into its deck, moving on with faux urgency.

Brilliant, but lazy.

Those words described him too well. Then it dawned on Victor—maybe there was more to life than misanthropy and elitism. He pushed it aside, like he did all inconvenient epiphanies, but the thought lingered. Victor was meant for greatness—he'd said it a thousand times over. But then, why was he here, amongst the squalor he so despised?

Maybe I'm not so different.

Regardless, he shuddered to think of himself as one cog in the machinations of humanity. He was as far from great as one could get, except in his dreams. Amongst the haze, all ambiance was unfamiliar, distortions of suburban noise, making him ponder who or what lay hidden, while beyond lay a weird

15

light, that aria echoing still.

And yet, Victor felt something was *off* this time.

A wicked laugh echoed through the twilight as a phantom emerged from the mist, fresh out of medieval poetry, and not quite human. Whether angel or devil, he could not say.

What the hell is this...?

Victor took a step back, recognizing that laughter as his own. Indeed, he saw his own face in the figure's, only for it to morph into a venetian mask of silver.

"Dude, Victor!" a familiar voice called. "What are you up to?"

Victor snapped out of deep thought and spun around, seeing Charles Garner emerging from the mist. As a middle-aged hipster, his style was an acquired taste. He was dressed in a tie-dye tee under a deep green peacoat. Below his peace belt buckle and '70s Walkman were cowboy boots and denim jeans. His face was like Colonel Sanders with tea shades, grayish-blond hair pulled back into a ponytail, utilitarian yet nonetheless "groovy."

"Weird weather, huh?" He looked about, adjusting his glasses with a sniff.

Victor said nothing—he was not in the mood. He took one last look at the cathedral. He saw nothing else, but remembered the Opera House and those warning words.

Charles looked concerned. "You all right?"

"I'm fine."

"Bullshit." Charles rolled his eyes. "You look like someone ran over your puppy."

Victor stared into the groves, still pondering the nature of this predicament.

"What're you looking at?" Charles joined in the staring. "What's up?"

Victor tried to formulate his thoughts into words, but his attempts fell utterly flat. "I'm not sure I can explain it," he began. "You know how I meditate sometimes, right?"

"Yeah, I knew a few Buddhists way back who did that."

"What would you say if I told you that—when I do, really deeply, I see things."

"Uh...." Charles ran his fingers through his hair. "What do you see, man?"

Victor showed Charles his symphonic sketches. "Can you sight read?"

"Fuck, man," he scoffed. "You know I barely played piano."

"Right, right...sorry." Victor cleared his throat and sung the overture, but by the look on Charles's face, it sounded better on paper. "Anyway, it's based on my dreamscape—"

"Is your dreamscape by chance the lovechild of Hendrix and Wagner? Because it seriously sounds like it." Charles paused, no doubt realizing his poor choice of words. "Hey, didn't mean it like that." He looked about, a glimmer of paranoia in his eyes, and pulled out a smoke. Whether spliff or cigarette, Victor didn't really care. "You mind?"

Victor smiled. "I'll take that as a compliment though." He stared into the distance. "Ever since I was little, I dreamed of this other world, if that makes sense. This afternoon, I had a nightmare. I was in this concert hall, there was this force, and—I hope they're just hallucinations. I can't help but wonder."

"That's...." Charles stared at him in disbelief, his smoke sticking out like a farmer's straw. "I don't even know. Did you take your Zoloft?"

"Yeah." Victor stared back into the grove. "But this makes me think about matters on an existential level. You know, cosmic scale philosophy, relating humanity to the stars and beyond, how one man fits into the boundlessness of reality, and—"

17

"I know what existentialism is." Charles rolled his eyes. "I'm the one who made you take that philosophy class, asshole."

Victor's eyes shifted away. "Sorry."

"You mean, like 'is any of this for real' and stuff. Solipsism?"

"More or less, but that's more metaphysical than existential."

"Well...." Charles dropped his charred end, grinding it into wet cobblestone. "I think I know what you need. Want to go to Gerald's and get some cheese and beer?"

Victor held back a smile. "Sure. Why not?" He calmed down. "You're a good friend, Charles. Thank you."

"Hey, a friend in need's a friend indeed —"

"But a friend with weed is better?" Victor smirked.

"You know me too damn well, dude."

#

Once past the oaken doors, Victor smelled parmesan and IPAs almost instantly. Most bars were deafening nightclubs, but they were men of taste, at least they liked to think so. Gerald's at G Street was a classier place, having the only cheese selection Victor didn't scoff at. They pulled a seat and ordered their usual — a pitcher of malty beer and a double crème platter. Charles was a boisterous drinker, draining his first in less than two minutes.

"Some things never change." Victor took a sip.

Charles covered his mouth as he belched, and retorted, "Please. If there's one thing I taught you, it's that nothing cures an existential crisis like a cold one. I would know." His eyes widened as he noticed something. "Hang on, is this a chess table?"

Victor glanced down and indeed saw a chessboard, complete with two drawers containing the respective pieces.

"I'll play you," they said almost simultaneously, before laughing and setting up the game.

"Of course, you picked black," Charles said. "You're more goth than geek, man."

"I always choose black," Victor replied. "Your move."

As the game continued they engaged in small talk, something Victor only enjoyed with Charles. Despite their differences, he found they complemented each other. Without Charles, he would be an unsociable pariah, and in turn, he'd taught Charles the beauty of classical music. Before long, the two were making "dick jokes" and debating who was worse, Tojo or Stalin.

"Checkmate." Charles flicked over the blackthorn king. "Jesus, you really suck."

"I have no gift for strategy," Victor acknowledged. "Right brain and all that."

Meanwhile, the bar had grown crowded, and Victor fiddled with the cards.

"Tarot?" Charles gave him a cock-eyed look. "I didn't know you bought into that."

"I don't," Victor said. "I-it's just an heirloom, seriously."

Charles sighed, smiling to himself. "I remember last time I got mine read. I was what, sixteen? Got the Magician Arcana, for some reason. But doesn't it mean like, energy and leadership? And initiative? Or...."

As Charles rambled on, Victor finished a fourth beer, until he recognized someone nearby. "Beatrice?!" he sputtered. "W-what's she doing here?"

Beatrice sat in the corner, oblivious to them, sketching on thick paper with some charcoal. Her skin was smooth under her clothing—a Sisters of Mercy T-shirt, cleavage on display, with dark jeans and platform boots, and pinned-up hair.

Like a modern Bettie Paige.

"Oh, that's her name? Hell if I know." Charles finished his

sixth, and let loose another belch, not bothering to cover his mouth. "I spend more time playing 'dem vidya games than wit' women, you know that. My last girlfriend was in '95."

"Is she looking over here?"

"Why?" Charles punched his arm harder than he probably meant. "You into her?"

Victor rubbed his bicep. "What if I am? We aren't in middle school."

"We sure as hell act like it," Charles said. "Go talk to her."

Victor gave him a stupefied look. "You, sir, are drunk."

"So?" Charles shrugged and took another swig, glasses lopsided. "You're young and allowed to do that shit." He squinted at her. "Roll against hotness, brother, you're gonna need it."

Victor's vision was so blurred, he could not tell if she was looking back. "She's smoking, like Pompeii before its eruption." He got up, bottle in hand. "And know what? I'm going to talk to that beautiful, alluring, young, beautiful—"

"All talk, man." Charles stifled a chuckle. "Seriously, when you're my age, talking doesn't get you far. Sooner or later, you'll have to just do it. Otherwise, you'll end up like me, wishing for a pile of money under a pile of titties, and a diploma."

They burst into idiotic laughter, drawing the attention of most people, including Beatrice. When he regained his senses, Victor turned around to see her walking towards them, boots clomping as the world slurred, his stomach dropped, and his heart began palpitating.

"Hey." She tried to smile. "I didn't know you drank."

"Oh." Victor ran his fingers through his hair. "I drink, all right. When I drink, my friends know I'm drunk."

Beatrice tried to hold back pity-filled laughter, but Victor brushed it off as a compliment.

"Would you like to join us?" He turned to Charles, only to find him haphazardly rolling a spliff, while looking over his shoulder in an anxiety-fueled stupor.

"Do you have a ride to the dorms?" Beatrice ignored Charles. "I have a bike."

Victor waved his hand. "I'm fine." He leaned on a barstool, trying to look cool while trying not to keel over. "Do you come here often?"

"Oh my god." Beatrice winced with disdain.

"Hmm?" He did not hear her.

"Oh, nothing." She tried to smile. "Really though, you're trashed. It's like you're begging to get mugged. The streets aren't exactly safe this damn late."

"Then, what would you suggest?"

"That you let me drive you back to campus."

"Ah!" Victor pointed his index fingers like revolvers. "I see, you're coming on to me!" He twiddled his thumbs. "Just as planned."

"I was. You seemed nice and kind of nerdy, until you started acting like a socially challenged frat boy." She patted Victor's back. "It's okay. I can take your friend home too."

#

The three stumbled out the door, trying not to knock each other over, Beatrice practically holding them upright. Victor was blinded by streetlamps and thickening fog, and he saw a weird light in the bar's television, reminding him of that dream. But he shrugged it off as a trick of liquor.

"Okay, guys." Beatrice gestured down the sidewalk. "My bike is there."

"Bike?" Victor did not understand, distracted by nothing. "You mean like a—bicycle."

"Yes, Victor." Beatrice radiated with sarcasm. "I ride a

21

bicycle on the freeway. No. I ride a motorcycle. It's way more badass than a car. I can still fit you both."

Charles, having fallen behind, staggered after them. "Guys, wait up!"

She guided Charles back to the sidewalk. Sure enough, they came to a parking garage in mere minutes and found Beatrice's motorcycle—riveted and decorated with a cobra seat and chrome pipework, and large enough to hold three people, counting the sidecar.

Its license plate read, DRAGULA.

"All right." Beatrice hopped on and revved the engine. "Who wants shotgun?"

The next thing he knew, Victor was clinging onto Beatrice's waist for dear life, while Charles stared wide-eyed in terror from the right. The cold night air swept through Beatrice's bangs. She smiled, zipping down the avenues and onto the freeway.

Victor, despite his drunken haze, felt like he was in some high-speed nightmare, squeezing the driver as tight as he could without actually hurting her.

"I wish I'd walked," he muttered in a maddened mantra. "I wish I'd walked."

Victor wondered just how often "bikes" crashed near the interstate, drivers mutilated in an inferno of metal and gasoline. He shuddered and glanced at the speedometer.

80 MPH

"Having fun?!" Beatrice shouted as loud as she could.

"No!" was all he could muster.

She laughed and slowed down to sixty-five.

At this barely tolerable and legal speed, he tried to see something beyond the surrounding fog, only to hear something truly uncanny. First came a wail on the wind, a noise no vehicle could make. Victor glanced over his shoulder, eyes wide.

Some cars stopped in mid-lane, others accelerated beyond the possible, as the concrete and yellow lines warped in the mist.

And then, a rift between two worlds ruptured.

Victor's hold slipped and he looked away, almost falling onto the pavement. Beatrice swerved to the side, piloting the bike carefully so as not to send them flying. But in mid-turn, Victor gazed in horror as a truck's headlights closed in, its horn drowned by the cries of his panic, and for a time, he saw only whiteness, ears ringing with a familiar voice.

I warned you, clearer than day, but you did not listen. Now you must pay the price, for darkness has descended. Dreams are just as important as reality, and now your perception is obscured by the fog of pride and denial. But how you react is your choice alone.

"Victor?" Beatrice's voice rang past the delirium. "Victor!"

He snapped back to reality, lying next to the sputtering motorcycle, Beatrice and Charles looming over him. It was clear what he saw, and it wasn't a hallucination.

Charles stared in shock, beginning to sober up. "You—you're not dead!"

Victor tried to speak but found himself at a loss for words. Time had stopped, the city sights obscured by billowing mist, save for its source—a ripple in reality, all churning and ethereal, a vortex of darkness and starlight, nearer than it looked.

"What *is* that?" Charles stared at the black hole, and from its threshold came a melody of twisted metal in G minor. "V-Victor," he stuttered. "What is that?"

"I...," Victor choked. "I don't know. But I think it's calling to me."

"Calling to you?" Beatrice came to his side. "What the fuck are you talking about?"

"My God," Charles chuckled, as if trying to lighten the mood, though something was wrong. Horribly wrong. "This

23

was real for you, and now — real for us?"

"Real for us?" Beatrice's voice tightened. "What kind of shit is that?! This has to be some kind of mass hysteria or something! This is just a bad accident, and — "

Suddenly, a shrieking chord filled the air, echoing from the toppled bike's radio, and Victor turned his head. His own shadow extended into the rift, where doll masks floated in a pool of oozing ichor, all roiling and viscous, their bodies slowly rising.

Charles's jaw dropped, and he took a step back. "What the — ?"

The shadows charged towards Victor with infernal cries, as if drawn to his terror. He felt someone tackle him, and the next thing he knew, Beatrice loomed over him.

"Run." She flipped a combat knife from her boot stop, kneeling. "Run!"

Victor hoisted himself up. This was his chance — but then what? Hide in his apartment? Drift deeper into madness? No. This was a darkness of his own making. Victor felt something in his pocket again, the Moon Arcana, the omen of dreams and fantasy, igniting another possibility, opening the way to a road less traveled.

"I...." Victor pinched the cards desperately. "Brave or stupid. I need to know."

At that moment inky tentacles swept him up, tossing him into the portal before Victor could even scream. In his petrification, all peeled away to a maelstrom of deepest fog, where stars were warped towards a funnel's end. At the end was an eye, its gaze unblinking and unrelenting, like the lens of a cosmic camera. And so, Victor saw reality's threads thin, cast into whatever lay beyond, blinded by nothingness, until the voice returned.

Welcome to your innermost world.

CHAPTER THREE

The year was 1884, by Imperial reckoning, for this far land was not of the Waking World.

Dawn never came to Holy Gothica, the City with the Iron Sky, and it was The Inquisition's duty to keep it so. Within a fog of ill omen, Ser Hector Thaddeus knelt before the corpse of a prostitute, fishnets and lace strewn about, a doll mask stitched to her face. She had been found and reported as, "impaled on a broadcasting pole," like all the others. He tested her wounds with holy water — it sizzled on contact. Something unholy had murdered the serf.

"Men shall die for this," he muttered. "That I promise."

Though bald and ebony, Thaddeus's limbs were of metal and wheels, far stronger than flesh. Above a brass respirator his eyes were cold and piercing, as tubes jutted from his neck, cabled to the engine fused to his lungs. He was dressed in a military uniform under a trench coat, yet wore the hat of a witch hunter. Across his back was an electro-staff of chrome and copper, topped with a raven, while hanging from his belt was a sword of blessed iron — both were the arms of a paladin sworn to the Third Gothic Imperium, right or wrong.

Truly, these are dire times.

Thaddeus watched as bystanders quickly looked away, moving down the bustling streets. He shook his head. If only they understood the price he paid to keep security. Of his own virtue he was justly proud, and Thaddeus tried to see the same in everyone, but in a totalitarian state, sometimes punishing the guilty came before protecting the innocent.

Such is my charge. My burden.

He counted the remaining hours until he could go home to his townhouse on Bosch Street, enjoying the Circus of Hours by his happy lonesome. But as he brushed the filth off his coattails, he heard something in the distance, a vomitous moan. Thaddeus drew his sword and turned to the alley, his fluorescent eyes shining in the darkness, as something cast a shadow.

"Ugh," a familiar voice wheezed. "Why did I sign up for this? I'd almost rather be back pushing pens. You know I can't stand the sight of blood."

"How long are you going to act like a conscript?" Thaddeus's words reverberated from the speaker on his throat. "I almost killed you then and there, Leng, thinking you were a leper."

"Heh, nope." The shadow stood upright, wiping his face with a handkerchief. "But if this keeps up, it wouldn't surprise me if the plague takes the city." Walter Leng came forward as lamplight shimmered off his greasy hair. He was awkward, with a monkish raincoat over a suit and tie, punctuated by a lazy slouch. He was clean-shaven, his wan fingers never far from the revolver on his side. "Damn," the deputy wheezed. "Sorry about that. Same case, I take it?"

"Indeed." Thaddeus lowered his blade, turning to the corpse. "The third victim since mid-Martus. All in a month's time." He sighed. "Pitiable. No doubt she died in terror, butchered by our murderer. I pray this harlot is absolved for her sins, and passes to the Kingdom of Ends."

"Yeah, ditto." Leng came to his side, eyes glued to a ledger filled with calligraphic prayers. "Any new leads or suspects? This has been going for a while, hasn't it?" He gagged again, as if catching a whiff of death. "Do you know?"

"Not until we check the Vox Networks." Thaddeus sighed. "For all our industry, we can't even track down this psychopath." He laid a hand on his forehead. "I am missing something."

"What I don't get is, why the telephone poles?" Leng sighed, pondering. "I mean, can you imagine the hassle it takes to put a body up there? I know our systems malfunction during the surges. But still, I can't think of how anyone can do that."

"Those blackouts will be the death of us. Black magic, I warrant," Thaddeus said. "Whenever the Cacophony creeps from realms chthonic, these murders are soon to follow." He turned to the pole. "I do not understand, Leng, why this is happening."

"Personally, I think someone is taking advantage of the Vox Networks." Leng shrugged. "They could hijack the power grids and rewire the ducts. But, hey, I'm just speculating."

There was a screech of static from all around. As Leng whipped out a riveted codec, turning a few dials, Thaddeus stepped forward and there was a burst of radiance above, a rift of alien smoke and fire. It shrieked and wailed, but as it vanished, they saw something descend to earth like a mist bound comet, landing a full district away.

"Leng." Thaddeus stared on, transfixed. "Check the Vox-logs. Notify the Stormtrooper Corps."

"I'm on it." Leng adjusted a knob and several images appeared, photographs taken from the many surveillance cameras. "Wait. It's human. No identity brand, either."

"Though to call it strange would be a gross understatement," Thaddeus said, "I have my hands full as it is. Surely another agent shall—"

A metallic ping echoed from the codec's speaker, and Leng skimmed a digital telegram. "Funny you mention that." He shut the handheld device. "Looks like we've been reassigned on a manhunt too. Come on, best not keep the witch-pyres cold."

"You cannot be serious." Thaddeus glowered. "They honestly think this is more important than hunting down a serial killer? I have spent nearly a month investigating these murders, and now you are telling me to drop that for some outsider?"

"We have our orders." Leng shrugged. "Who knows, the guy might be touched by something eldritch. You remember that other rift, right? Just a month ago, too. Two figures were detected, only to vanish in mere days. No leads. Anyway, he landed near Serfdom One."

"What is he doing there? The entire district will be under curfew in two hours."

"I don't know." Leng sighed. "But listen, the Ecclesiarchy just ordered us to track him down and bring him in for interrogation, and probably exorcism. Since that's *your* talent."

Thaddeus stared at the Iron Sky, to fool himself that the state's angels watched from steel heavens. No matter what he'd like to believe, he knew the proper protocol.

"Very well. Let us hurry and find him before the Thirteenth Frequency airs." Thaddeus turned to the Imperial Court. "I only hope there is an end to this trail of blood."

#

When Victor's eyes rolled open, he wondered if he was still "hallucinating," waking in a dark alley. Staggering upright, he felt bits of cobblestone fall off his back, as if he had plummeted from a great height. Miraculously, he was unharmed. Taking a few shaky steps, Victor peered down the city narrows, where lamplight shone on a dim way, only to pause before its end.

Oh my God!

Cathedrals and citadels loomed over avenues and alleys, lined with ductworks and drains. Locomotives whistled above the streets, while gin and gun smoke reeked from the taverns, all in a haze of misery. The Iron Sky bolted out the true heavens, locking the populace in here with plate and pipe, as monastic chants, like something Victor would compose, played over radios.

Whether this was a different time or another planet, he did not know — he knew only that his home did not exist on its atlas.

Like a goth's Orwellian nightmare.

Then he heard a sharp whirr and spun around, heart leaping up his throat. Nestled between supports, a mechanical gargoyle stared at him with zooming lenses, as if part of some surveillance system. Mustering his wits, Victor shuffled down the street, paranoid, voices of bystanders ringing in his skull. Its people were a motley lot, ranging from beggars to punks and youths. The latter were most interesting, their fashion a quilt of long coats and studded leather.

"Who the hell is that? Never seen him before."

"What kind of getup is he in?"

"Poor bastard's begging to get taken in."

As the world spun, Victor tried to put on his headphones, but the venomous glances of passersby made him think otherwise. The reeks of factory smoke and unwashed bodies made him gag, but as the moments dragged on, Victor could barely *hear* anything, panic welling in his chest until he was about to scream. Then it hit him, and Victor halted and paled.

Charles…Beatrice. Where are you?

His breathing tightened, staring at this darkest metropolis. One thing was clear—Victor needed to find his friends. If they were here, they couldn't be far. And so he waded deeper into the city. The ghettos loomed inward, stacked as towering, teetering blocks, signs flashing with kanji-like script. They were packed and dense, reeking of rotten fish and sewage, paper lanterns swaying in the mist, every road leading to, "Yoshiwara District."

This city is massive.

In the ethnic quarters, Victor wandered about the sushi carts and street peddlers until he saw a tremendous, triple-tiered pagoda on the horizon, laced with scarlet paper lanterns. He was dazzled by those sights, until such implications hit him.

Is that a red light district?

"Hey," a feminine voice asked. "You all right there?"

Victor looked over his shoulder, and saw a young woman leaning against a streetlamp. Her hair flowed in scarlet locks, and her ivory skin glistened in the dimness. Dressed in a peacoat and fishnets, she lit a clove with the flick of a lighter.

"O-oh!" Victor stammered. "I'm...." His eyes locked with hers, if only for a moment. They were green and glittering. Fluorescent, even. "F-fine," he finished.

"Lost, huh?" She puffed, giving a coy smile, revealing her stitched lips. "Yeah, you're too highbrow to be from around here. But if you're looking for a room, can't say I'd object."

Is she even human...? Still....

"A room?" Victor's mind raced with conflicting thoughts. He'd watched enough *film noir* to know when a prostitute was flirting with him. He shoved his hands into his pockets. "N-no, thank you. I'm afraid I haven't any money. I h-hope you understand."

One of many reasons.

31

"Of course." There was a twinge of disappointment in her voice.

"Well, I b-better get going," he said

"If you ever change your mind...." The streetwalker cocked her head towards the pagoda. "There's almost always a vacancy."

Victor bit his lip. "Thanks...."

She came to his side. "You'd like a sample, at least?"

"A *what*—?"

The streetwalker's lips pressed against his. Her tongue slid into his mouth, briefly. Victor moaned in shock—until he tasted dark chocolate and raspberries, muscles melting in her touch. With that she parted and slid past Victor, laying a hand on his chest.

"Have a good night," she whispered.

Victor spun around. Strange fog wafted from the pipes, obscuring the streetwalker as she walked away, heels clomping into the distance. He could still smell her lilac perfume, until—

What the!

He was crippled by sudden fatigue, almost slumping to his knees. A shrill, staticky buzz wormed into his mind, wreathing it in a miasma of confusion. Out of the corner of his eye he saw cobalt flame and his own rising shadow. A wicked laugh filled the air, and then—silence.

The streetwalker had vanished into the night. Victor was alone again.

He continued down the narrows, aimlessly.

In an alleyway, Victor saw a weathered cart draped in velvets and gilded fabrics, tasseled with bells and windchimes— somewhere between an ice cream truck and a gypsy caravan— pulled by an automated stallion of clockworks and black steel. As he stepped closer, Victor bumped into someone, sputtering,

"Oh...! So sorry."

A rigid arm pinned him against the wall. Eyes wide, Victor saw a hulk of a man in a hood and cloak, inches from his face. Ill-proportioned and lumbering, he gave a guttural rasp, and Victor caught a glimpse of a deformed face, jawless, drooping like molten wax.

My God!

"Brutus!" A blackthorn cane came between them. "There is no need for that."

The hulk obeyed at once, shambling back, and Victor heard sharp clatters on the ground. Something fell from Brutus's robes. Out of instinct, Victor picked up the trinkets — wooden blocks of ornate font, an ark carved from petrified oak, and a yo-yo, all crafted with artisanship.

Toys?

Brutus tugged at his hood with a groan, masking his face. The closer Victor looked, the more that cloak resembled an oversized security blanket, threadbare with childish patterns. The hulk's companion outstretched his fingers with a grin, as if trying too hard to be friendly.

"Here." Victor handed them over, hands shaking. "You dropped these."

"Thank you." He was a thin man of mundane features — muddy eyes and a mole on his brow — and yet, was dressed in a waistcoat of pink and pastel blue stripes, with gray slacks, suspenders, and shined shoes. Victor felt a sad yet sinister vibe past that smile — an embittered soul filled with pain. "My apologies." His eyes shifted. "My brother is more than a bit protective. You must understand, what with the killer on the loose."

"D-did you make those?" Victor eyed the blocks. "They're quite well-done."

33

"Thank you," the man repeated. "Your pardon, I am Edgar Munchausen. And it is our trade and mission to spread a little joy to the children in these slums." He passed the toys back to Brutus, who shoved them into the slots of a bulging pack amongst protruding stacks of saltwater taffy. "Don't be rude," he snapped. "Give him a lolly. You owe him that much."

Brutus gave an apologetic whimper, offering Victor an old-fashioned sucker.

"Uh." Victor took it with caution. "T-thanks."

"Where are you headed, young ser?" Edgar asked. "The taverns are closing soon."

Victor's mouth ran dry, trying to think of a "destination."

"Regardless, the Inquisition doesn't take to curfew violators any better than lepers." Edgar shuddered, looking away. "Try not to stay out late. Not tonight."

"Oh." Victor glanced down. "Thank you for the advice. And the—treat."

"Just telling truths, young ser." He pulled out a wallet and handed Victor a business card. "Well, we better be off too." He broke a softer smile as Brutus shambled back to the caravan. "Come by our shops if you want to see more. All who are young at heart are welcome."

Victor glanced at the printed card.

MUNCHAUSEN CANDY CO.
TOYS, TRINKETS, AND MORE.

He was about to thank the strangers, but when Victor looked up, Edgar and Brutus were already driving away as their hurdy-gurdy tune played into the night. He had no choice but to carry on.

Wandering the alleys, Victor turned to the news broadcasts on televisions behind the broken windows. Strangely enough, it was all live sermons and fog forecasts.

"As such, expect curfew to be enforced an hour earlier than usual," the newswoman said, voice gritty behind the speakers. "Please remember to keep your machinery locked and off. This is for your own safety. Everyone must play their part during the midnight surges—"

Then, all the televisions went black with a firm click.

Victor took a step back as the streetlamps flickered and the fog closed in. He was about to turn away when static blared from the speakers. Despite this blackout the screens flashed on, tuned to dead channels, and yet, something could be seen beyond that haze—a figure trapped behind the screen, silent but screaming. Not far away the people moved on, not even turning their heads, but whether blinded by mist or willfully oblivious, Victor could not say.

What is this?

He outstretched his trembling fingers, touching the glass of the nearest screen, only for it to ripple like a pool of warm water. As the buzzing grew louder, a scream became audible. Victor jerked his hand back, covering his ears, as a lamp blew a fuse with a sizzling bang. And then, there was only silence. Did only he see that? Regardless, Victor was harrowed by what had happened, his knees shaking. And while the people went on, oblivious, dread did not leave him.

A robotic monotone announced, "Curfew will begin in one hour."

Victor's heart skipped a beat, his pace quickening to a sprint, trying to find a haven amongst the slums. The broadcasts blared every fifteen minutes until the streetlights dimmed at last, and Victor was alone in the dark. Little lived in this no-man's land save for those crouched in alleys and shacks, damned to fester in these ghettos.

W-what the fuck?!

An air raid siren blared, and Victor was crippled by cold sweats and fatigue as something buzzed in his mind's ear. His vision glazed over with static, the antennae loomed and leered in the gaslight, and he slumped to his knees. There was a blinding flash, but as everything cleared, Victor felt something trickle on his brow, warm and sticky.

Oh...oh God.

Legs quivering, he stood up, slack-jawed. It was a doll-masked corpse, impaled on a telephone pole. His stomach sank like a boulder in a pool of molasses as music played in his mind's ear, an ominous piano piece playing the same chords over and over.

A gunshot jolted him. Victor spun around to see a squad of stormtroopers charging forth with rifles and bayonets, grim and gas-masked, coattails fluttering—something out of a wartime milieu. He sprinted as fast as his legs would carry him. Shouts obscured by rebreathers, the stormtroopers fired, but Victor was far too jerky a target, bolting from alley to alley, jackboots never far behind. But then he was tackled, skull crashing with a crack against the cobblestones.

He fell, dazed, staring into soulless goggles, and all faded to blackness.

#

Victor drifted in and out of consciousness. He felt music tingle within, interrupting his synapses with the aria from the Opera House once more. And for a time, he knew peace and reassurance.

But it was not to last.

His eyes jerked open as the music blurred into chants of confession. He was strapped to a chair in some interrogation cell. The stormtroopers stood beyond the barred door, all Stahlhelms and trench coats. The floor was of concrete, the walls lined with ducts, like the bowels of a boiler. Then the soldiers marched aside, making way for someone else.

"Ser Walter Leng," a Kaiser-helmed captain spoke, her voice firm yet venerating. "The men and I are honored by the Inquisition's presence."

"Can the formalities," a youthful voice wheezed. "Let's just get this shitshow over."

"I advise that you at least act your part," the captain replied. "I know it's against your nature. But we all have our duty for Empress and Ecclesiarchy."

"Yeah, you're right." Leng glanced at his pocket watch. "Are the preparations set? The labori accounted for? Is this the murder suspect?"

"Yes, ser," the captain said. "The 105th found him and reported to me. He has been unconscious for nearly two hours. No identification or anything of the sort, except for a deck of tarot cards. According to our records, the boy does not exist." She paused. "Doesn't that strike you as odd? Only a month has passed since the other incident, when the sky also rained fire."

"That's another reason why he's here." Leng glanced through the bars. "Damn, he's younger than me. Sad, but it's our job. Well, time to play good cop-bad cop." He cleared his throat. "Labori, stand ready."

#

The door opened and Leng emerged into the light, squinting at the overhead lamp. He pulled up a chair, flanked by a pair of robotic assistants—or robots, they seemed to be, for Victor saw bits of skin and sinew amongst their steel, as still-living machines of muscle and steroids. Collared and leashed, reeking of burnt oil, they were surgical monstrosities. He shuddered, for though Leng tried to smile, his gaze was unrelenting.

"W-where am I?" Victor's head was still a bludgeoned blur.

"Who are you people?"

"Yeah, you don't get to ask questions." Leng straightened a stack of wrinkled files, and the labori clamped their claws around Victor's biceps. "Consider this your interrogation. We're here to judge whether or not you're guilty of...."

All was a haze of fright until Victor's mind jolted to the present, labori tightening their grips, threatening to snap his arms in two. He flinched, but Leng was still calm and friendly.

"Come on." The inquisitor cocked an eyebrow. "I asked you a question. Take a deep breath." He rummaged through his pockets, offering Victor a flask. It stank of gin. "Who are you? Be honest, please. It'll save us time, and you a great deal of pain."

Victor's mouth was dry. Even if he'd known how to answer, his dignity cried out against it. What good would it do him? He'd probably wind up burned at the stake either way. But the threat of torture and death was persuasive enough.

"U-uh," he stammered. "M-my name is Victor Roland. I'm n-not from here."

"Okay." Leng scribbled down a few notes. "That's kind of obvious, so I can't say I don't believe you. And since you aren't from here, let me make a few things clear." He laid an unfamiliar badge on the table. "Do you know what this is?"

Victor shook his head.

"It is an iron rosette, and with it, I may execute as many souls as I deem necessary, delivering them to the Pearly Gates for judgment." His eyes glimmered for a moment. "But I have never had to use it. Not once. That said, the Inquisition is clandestine and paramilitary, bound by no other authority. Now, where do you come from?"

"It's—weird," Victor mustered a reply. "I feel like I've been here before. In another time. It's like something out of a dream.

I *fell* down here. This can't be real."

"*Fallen?*" Leng's eyes flashed with curiosity. "Something out a dream?"

"Leng." A broadcast blared on the cell intercom, its voice mechanical yet human. "I will meet you at Cell Block 218 in five minutes."

"Fuck." Leng looked away. "Hang in there." He stood up. "Just remember I'm the good cop, and I'll be back." His face paled a bit. "I'll tell Thaddeus what I know; hopefully he'll go a little easier on you. Just try not to bleed everywhere, okay?"

With that Leng left the room, whether for minutes or hours Victor could not tell, with his heart pounding in his ears, alone with the dead eyes and iron masks of the labori. What heinous tortures awaited him? All in the name of false confession, and —

"In the name of our hallowed Fog-Bringer." A laugh echoed from a nearby cell, like a madman locked in an asylum. "We shall —"

"Silence," yelled a guard, followed by a buzzing saw and a bloodcurdling scream. "Enough of your heresy! You'll be taken to the firing squad before dawn. Give him his last rites!"

Even those noises faded in due time. The door swung open and in marched Ser Hector Thaddeus, a man of iron hands and iron will, as announced by the captain outside.

"Interesting." Thaddeus scanned Leng's notes. "You believe this is a dream, and have no recollection of this world." He stared at Victor. "Delusional or not, you are an outsider — this is apparent. But what were you doing near Yoshiwara, violating state curfew? Where so many have gone missing?" He leaned in close. "Choose your next words carefully, Victor."

"W-what is there to explain?" he stammered. "I know this is about that body — I'm not a moron. But if you think I did it, you have the wrong guy! I barely remember what happened."

"If you can't give a straight answer...." Thaddeus unrolled a set of bloody tools of torture, gnarled and serrated. "Then I shall extract one of my own."

The door burst open, and Leng rejoined the interrogation.

"U-uh, Thaddeus," he stuttered. "I think—"

"Hold your tongue." Thaddeus prepared a joint-breaking crank. "You are not qualified to handle these affairs, due to your hemophobia." He turned to Victor. "You have nothing to fear if you have nothing to hide. Know that, and this will be painless."

"Oh, come on." Leng stifled his frustration, however callous. "You know that's bullshit in practice. If you don't believe him, you'll just keep at it until he dies. You know what I'm getting at. Trust me, this isn't our guy."

"Then explain your hypothesis, and make it succinct for once."

"Don't worry, it's relevant." Leng laughed nervously. "Remember, we had another sighting." He withdrew his codec, turning a few dials, until a distorted image appeared on its convex screen. "And look! No identity brand. Just like Mr. Roland here." He turned to Victor. "You said you'd fallen through something? Because that something also appeared here, and our scanners went off the charts." He nodded at Thaddeus. "We found this guy, what—an hour after these readings? If you want my hypothesis, he's no killer. He's something else."

Victor shivered. "Something else? Then why am I here?"

"Hell if I know." Leng crossed his arms, seemingly pleased with himself. "I'm not saying we should let him go. Something's up, but it's not murder."

Thaddeus remained stoic and silent.

"Hey, think about it." Leng's smile faded. "What would *she* say?"

"That was a poor choice of words." Thaddeus stood, hand falling upon a pouch on his utility belt. "And yet, in times like these, we should not bring judgment on our own." He emptied the pouch onto his palm, revealing a set of knuckle-bones, old and runic. "No urn or grave for my dearest. But I carry her with me, as a talisman, and I shall ask her —"

"Hey now." Leng's eyes shifted nervously. "Let's not gamble on this."

"There is no gamble, only fate." Thaddeus blessed his brow. "Shall I absolve this man? Or shall I condemn him, as codex and creed would have me?'

Victor shut his eyes as Thaddeus tossed the bones in the air, a hand over his sword. Although he was an outsider, as they said, Victor knew his fate resided in crude divination. He shivered with cold fear, and when the bones clattered on the table, his heart dropped. But when his eyes fluttered open, Thaddeus and Leng stared in awe.

"Well then," Leng scoffed.

"Indeed, it seems your death is not mine to warrant," Thaddeus concluded, rubbing his iron fingers against the bones. "Your descent is not without purpose. But whether good or ill, I cannot say." He straightened. "I shall transfer you to the Apostolic Palace, by sanction of Empress and Ecclesiarchy, to learn of your origins, as it were. But should you raise a finger against me, you will pay in blood."

As Thaddeus turned his back, Leng gestured for the labori to release Victor, much to his relief. The inquisitor offered him a hand, trying to smile. Victor was taken aback by the sweaty grip, and knew his misadventures were just beginning.

"Well, hang in there, okay?" Leng tried to comfort him, guiding him down the long hall. "Just don't try anything too stupid, and we're good."

41

CHAPTER FOUR

Curfew did not apply here, though few people dared linger in the shadow of the Palace of Justice. As the inquisitors escorted Victor along the prison's parapets, he halted atop a walkway in between the guard turrets, gazing across the slums of Serfdom Three. They formed a labyrinth of industrial ugliness as cooling towers loomed along the outer wall, their supports bracing the Iron Sky, casting a perpetual shadow over the City Below.

What kind of nightmare did I fall into?

"Come." Thaddeus gestured down a winding stairway to the courtyard and barred gates beyond. "A clerical train should stop nearby and take us to the Central Servitorium. We must board soon, if we are to reach the Apostolic Palace before dawn."

"Yeah." Leng cocked his head. "Let's get a move on, Victor."

The inquisitors walked on either side of him, never out of arm's reach. Thaddeus's rasping breath and clanking joints made Victor uneasy, reminiscent of serials and space operas.

"Quit staring," Thaddeus said. "It is quite rude."

Victor's eyes darted to the cobblestones, shuffling beside his captors.

As they left the fortress, walking down the streets in silence, they came across a newsstand, where an automaton tended to its tabloids and pulpy pages. It was like a wheeled can of tin and brass, bearing the Imperial Crest, flanked by skeletal arms. As Victor stared at the machine, the inquisitors muttered between themselves.

"What the hell is up with this kid?" Leng said. "He just appeared out of thin air."

"I know not," Thaddeus replied. "However, I suspect heresy, and...."

Their voices lowered and Victor was left to his own devices, if only for a moment. Desperate to learn something about this place, he waited until their backs were turned and snatched up an article.

REMEMBERING DOCTOR JOSEF MURDOCH

It has been one year since Dr. Murdoch's disappearance, and all can agree the world will not be the same. As the man behind Holy Gothica's Industrial Revolution, he discovered the alternating current, radio technology, the pictogram and motion pictures, and of course, the analytical engine, paving the way to our Age of Industry. However, one year ago, Dr. Murdoch returned from the [RECORD EXPUNGED] a broken man....

"Are you going to pay for that?" the automaton asked, its monotone like an old man over a transceiver. "It is a crime to read any work without first purchasing."

"Huh?" Victor did not understand, at first. "S-sorry...." He dug into his pockets, but only found a dime, a few buttons, and that lollipop from before.

"All's good." Leng stepped forward, sliding a few gear-shaped thalers into the automaton's coin slot. "I'll pay for him."

With that, he took another copy of the daily paper. "Let's go."

"T—thanks." Victor smiled, though a tad suspicious. "I appreciate it."

"Don't worry about it." Leng smiled back, rummaging through his pockets. "By the way...." He handed back Victor's tarot deck. "Cool cards. I got some like those."

"You believe in fortune telling?" Victor's brow furrowed, taking the heirloom back with shaky hands. "Isn't that heretical, or something?"

Leng shook his head. "The Imperial Tarot is all good. Originally it was just another tool of divination used by the gypsies. Then it really took off with the upper class, and became a popular set of playing cards here in the slums. How many cards in your reading?"

"Just one. The Moon. And you?"

"The Fool," Leng laughed. "Freedom and a pinch of chaos, first and foremost. But yeah, let's just say the brothels at Yoshiwara are my thing. Thaddeus over here got the Hierophant, or so I hear. Piety and fatherhood, mostly. I wonder why?"

"Enough. Midnight is almost upon us," Thaddeus growled, as a train whistled in the distance. "We must hurry, before the Thirteenth Frequency hits the radio systems."

The Thirteenth Frequency?

As they marched through the Cathedral Ward, Victor beheld statues of angels and saints, none of which he recognized, gesturing towards the Iron Sky. The greatest of all was an outlined figure, a vertical corpse against a clockwork cot, surrounded by grieving followers, like a hospitalized prophet of steam, it's placard reading,

THE FAR MESSIAH

In their shadows were confessional booths, where the masses shifted in single file, dressed in waistcoats and torn trousers, seeking forgiveness. Victor overheard pre-recorded sermons, preaching that only obedience would grant them the church-state's blessing. Such was the monopoly of faith. But as they moved on, Victor flipped through the pages of his newsletter, skipping to a "public safety" portion, trying to learn more without asking his wardens.

... As for the leprosy itself, no one knows its cause or cure, only that it corrodes the mind, reducing the infected to ravenous maniacs. We must remind you to report....

A draft of exhaust tossed about the pages until Victor could hardly read it. Only after smelling the smoke of tanneries did he realize —

"Ser?" A voice spoke from under his nose, wet and raspy. "Spare a few thalers?"

Victor looked about, only to find a panhandling leper by the sidewalk, dressed in rags and a tattered coat. A rusty bell dangled from her neck, and she smelled of sickly sweat and mildew. A mask of bandages drooped over the leper's face, but she smiled still, as much as one could, a bowl of motley change and a painted plank by her side, reading,

Smile. Life could always be worse.

Victor's stomach sank, wondering if the leper was contagious. He saw Leng move on, not even batting an eye. Then again, poverty seemed all too common. Who would judge Victor for turning his back? Only himself, and that was enough. But then, Thaddeus approached the leper and stared down. His hand lay on his sword hilt, the other digging into that belt pouch, and the leper's eyes widened in terror, until....

"Yes." The inquisitor dropped a platinum coin in the bowl. "I suppose it always could be worse." He bowed his head.

"Charity is part of the Ecclesiastical creed, after all."

"Bless you." The leper's blistered lips curled into a smile. "Maybe I can finally see the apothecary." She shifted the motley change in her bowl. "Thank you, sers."

"There are also sick houses upon the eastern outskirts of Serfdom Four," Thaddeus said. "I trust the vestals will take care of you. That coin shall surely pay for a basic treatment."

Another whistle pierced their ears from the tracks above, and Leng glanced at his pocket watch. "All niceties aside," he said, "we should get going, as you keep saying."

Victor saw a train stopping on a station overhead, a tube of iron supports and wire mesh atop elevated tracks. It was a diesel-powered engine of gray steel, modeled to resemble a series of segmented naves, lined with gargoyles and stained glass—a feat of engineering.

"Indeed." Thaddeus nodded, turning to the stairs. "Come, Victor."

#

The train took them past the churchly sights of the Cathedral Ward, but it soon crossed the grimy walls of Serfdom Four, and into the ravaged ghettos of its Leper Quarter. Victor tried to stare out the window, only to shudder at the perpetual fog. That unearthly chill shattered all joy and peace, and he felt evil germinating in the dimness.

"Hey." Leng broke the silence. "I know this looks horrible, but trust me, we aren't the bad guys. You know, Holy Gothica is just down on its luck. Has been for a while. And all despotism aside, the Ecclesiarchy really is just trying to make things better."

"How do you fit into all this? You're part of the secret police. You don't exactly have morality on your side." Victor shook his head. "Why am I even talking to you?"

46

Leng's smile faded. "Because you're still our prisoner. And don't go around placing us all in one box, especially when I'm trying to go easy on you." He glanced at Thaddeus, who was still reading his codex, unaware. "Some of us are a bit... unhinged, yeah. But you'll find that anywhere. I think the Grand Conductor is too busy running the next life to answer prayers, but that's where we come in. Kinda cool, huh?" He turned to Victor, only to be met with a glare. "Anyway, I'm just a curator, mostly. I keep an eye on Thaddeus. He has a record with 'summary executions.' The paperwork for that shit is abysmal."

The color faded from Victor's face. His mind raced with images of internment camps and police brutality — images that did not seem too farfetched here in Holy Gothica.

"S-summary executions?" he blurted. "What kind of dictatorship *is* this?"

Leng rolled his eyes. "Oh, you're one of *those* people. Well, it's one founded on necessity. I don't expect you to understand. But, if you're worried about getting shot, don't be. We're past the interrogation phase. Like I said, I keep Thaddeus wrapped up in red tape."

Victor was not convinced. He was nauseated with dread, and Leng's cavalier attitude was far from comforting. He dared not speak to Thaddeus, an ironclad shadow in the corner of his eye. But as his legs shivered, Victor remembered those relaxation techniques.

Deep breaths, Victor. Deep breaths....

As Leng rambled on, Victor noticed something rather odd about the inquisitor. Peeking from his pocket was an old-fashioned camera — portable, yet complete with a light and bellows.

"Oh." Leng raised the camera. "Curious about this?" He

smiled. "I used to be a filmmaker before joining the Inquisition. A memento from my dabblings in photography and the world of cinema. Quite an underrated industry, if you ask me."

"I am surprised the Ecclesiarchy let you keep it," Thaddeus grunted, peering from the pages of his codex. "Such art is a tool of the state. A tool that is easily misused."

"Please." Leng rolled his eyes. "It's just a token. I had some good times and some bad times, but I wouldn't trade those years for anything. Even got to walk the red carpet."

"I understand your 'dabbling' included pornography."

Leng smirked. "Any depictions of sexual perversion in *my* films can only be described as—educational." He lit another cigarette. "The Ecclesiarchy let me off damn easy, too."

Leng said no more, and Victor went about musical daydreams, trying to distract himself from overwhelming anxiety. But as his thoughts intensified, Victor heard a distant force mimic them—an orchestra echoing from the speakers of an ethereal television.

That was, until he saw that icon of oppression.

Battlement upon battlement, tier upon tier, the Phonos Engine loomed where the four serfdoms met, like an adamant fortress, supporting the Iron Sky with mighty buttresses, layered with ductworks. Those supports could swallow the steeples they shadowed, towering over the slums. All roads and power cables led to its machine-halls. The core pillar was covered in screens and two-bit clocks, broadcasting mental melodies from its transmitters.

"Oh." Leng turned the dials on his codec, until the same music played. "Never heard of the Symphonia Mundi?" The inquisitor shut his eyes. "Good music today."

"Yeah." Victor gazed across the city. "But what is it?"

"Thaddeus can probably explain it better than I can,

honestly." Leng turned to his colleague. "Would you mind letting him in on that?"

"And why would I do that?" Thaddeus cocked a cold eye. "He is not of the Imperium, let alone our faith. Why should we inform an outsider? Answer me that. Take care of the prisoner, for I will not." His voice lowered to a hiss. "I only hope there is a purpose behind all this."

Victor looked down, trying not to stare at the man of iron.

"Hey, kid," Leng whispered. "Don't be afraid of him. My job is—"

"I am crippled, not deaf, you fool, and I am not your servitor," Thaddeus interrupted. "Your charge is simple—to ensure my service to the Imperium, which is unconditional. You are unnecessary. Besides, I have more important things to deal with than you."

Leng glared at him. "*Unnecessary*? There's a reason you're on a leash. And crazy if you think I'm ever letting you off it. Yeah, remember when you went all gung-ho in that opium den? While we were undercover? When we had to blow up a whole textile facility? 'Cause the Central Servitorium sure does. It was a miracle they covered that shit up!" He sighed. "What's so damn important, anyway? Another one of your conspiracy theories?"

"I know the truth." Thaddeus clenched his fists, eyes glazed with frustration. "You heard in the Palace of Justice as well as I, Leng. The disturbed all speak of the 'Fog-Bringer,' and...." He loosened his grip. "Why do I bother? Men of science always forsake the wisdom of faith. All the murders occurred during the Thirteenth Frequency. It is when darkness reigns, and—"

"Wait, the surges?" Leng rambled. "I mean, sure, the world changes during the Devil's Hour. I'm not going to argue that. The Music of the Spheres becomes darker and interferes with our surveillance systems. But you're saying our Phonos Engine, finished less than a decade ago, has some direct impact on the metaphysical? That's like a bad urban legend."

As they argued, Victor stared out the window. He remembered the power outage and the figure behind the television screen. When his hand had plunged into its "glass," and that corpse had appeared not an hour later. Victor shuddered, and finally mustered the courage to speak up.

"I believe you." He did not look Thaddeus in the eye. "After what I've seen. I may not know the full truth, but I can guess."

"The truth." Thaddeus stared off, as if in debate. "If that really is what you seek, then you will heed my words. The radio and the television are more than technological achievements, Victor. They are windows into a dark, inner world—a sea of souls. Our memories and emotions send ripples across its aether, the Symphonia Mundi. Its exact nature is esoteric, but it cradles the heights of Heaven, and yet holds the depths of Hell beneath its wild currents and undertows. And its daemons are mirrors of the darkness in our hearts, opposing the Music of the Spheres—"

"Yeah," Leng chimed in. "That cymatic plane opens up when a very specific program is activated. We call it the Thirteenth Frequency, and it can only be detected if our systems go absolutely haywire. Think of it like a glitch."

Victor raised an eyebrow, trying to imagine a city running on the abstract.

"What, you don't think Holy Gothica runs on steam alone, do you?" Leng said. "When the music is manageable, we use it to power our complex machines, like the Phonos Engine. But if you believe in the Ecclesiarchy, you'd know they're drawn from the Grand Conductor's will."

"*If* you believe?" Thaddeus shot him a look. "Questionable

words for an inquisitor."

"Hey now, I'm just trying to be inclusive with the outsider." Leng returned the glare. "No need to get all pious on my ass. Besides, I still have your report to fill out. Don't forget."

"Without music life would be a mistake." Victor stifled a smile. "Very interesting."

Thaddeus did not reply, adjusting the knobs on his rebreather.

"Are there others out there?" Leng changed the subject. "Like you?"

Victor pondered for a moment. "Kind of. Two of them. It's weird. I haven't seen them since it all happened, but they can't be here too, can they?"

"It's possible." Leng shrugged. "One month ago there was a rift, and two outsiders apparated into existence. We couldn't find them. Nothing like that was ever recorded until then, but no harm has come from it. Strange, huh?"

"One month? They were with me when I fell. That makes no sense."

Could it be them, though?

A shriek of static burst from Leng's codec. The device smoked and sparked, and a rusty roar echoed below the train as it jerked to a halt.

"Goddammit!" He jumped and shut the handheld off. "Don't tell me we broke down!"

"I fear so." Thaddeus looked up as the lights flickered off. "Even if this railroad was not automated, no one would willingly stop here. We must go on foot."

Leng's jaw dropped. "But this is the Leper Quarter! We can't go outside!"

A dreadful silence passed. Thaddeus's electro-staff barely shone against the blackness.

"Stay close and do not stray." He stood up, tall and grim, drawing his sword and opening the door. A draft of thickfog smothered all light, leaving them alone in the dark. As whispers filled the air, Thaddeus led the plunge into the unknown. "Evil draws close."

CHAPTER FIVE

The city was fraught with droning dread, and Victor was trapped in a straightjacket of paranoia, struggling to no avail. The Phonos Engine loomed in the distance, its tower and screens glowing with gray light, dominating all as a bastion of eldritch evil.

And the rest of the city was not spared from its weirdness.

The Leper Quarter, a slum of faded and fetid colors on first glimpse, was now a grayscale haze of static and mist, a distorted mirror of an already wretched sight. The only things keeping their color were the antennae and their surroundings, and even they flickered against the fog, like beacons of fleeting hope. Meanwhile, lepers and soldiers stood motionless, transfigured into faceless statues in the night—the lost and the damned.

"W-what happened out here?" Victor asked. "Did time freeze?"

"In a manner. It is the Cacophony, the will of Hell, corroding reality in its nothingness, if only for a while," Thaddeus said. "Our engines, fueled by the Music of the Spheres, are most vulnerable to its evil. Its surges in the radio systems are a nuisance, but this is the effect of the Thirteenth Frequency—a true phenomenon when most technology ceases to function." He turned to the petrified statues. "And the weak of faith are left oblivious to its danger, when the line between this world and the next is thinned."

"I can't explain it any better," Leng said. "A full program that warps the city. It's like the world stops spinning, and strange energies spark into reality. Usually it hits at midnight, like a 'dead hour.' I don't know why, but few people remain conscious. It's why we have the curfew."

"That makes a lot of sense."

Leng managed a smile. "You seem surprised. Not all our laws are just to oppress the people, you know. Sometimes they actually work. Well, sometimes...."

Through the surreal haze Victor trailed after the inquisitors. As they marched through the fogbound slums, they came to a dilapidated building between the ghettos and the dark tower, Jericho Elementary School. Its windows were broken and boarded, its rooftop lined with barbed wire, gardens dry and dead, its sign marked with a bloodstained warning.

DANGER: QUARANTINE ZONE

"W-wait," Victor stuttered. "Quarantine zone?"

Leng took a few steps back. "We should go around."

Thaddeus pointed his blade forward. "I think not. This is the quickest way to the Central Servitorium. But this barrier was pushed back. This is not good."

"I don't care," Leng scoffed. "Quarantine zones are for the stormtroopers. Not us."

"Truly the words of a coward," Thaddeus retorted. "Go around if you are that frightened, but how long will you two last without me?" He creaked open the gate, pressing onward. "Should we be assailed, we shall fight hard and true. That I promise you."

54

Body shaking, Victor had no choice but to follow them.

#

The school's doorstep gave way to a maze of uncanny sights. Wandering from classroom to classroom, Thaddeus and Leng led the way, while Victor lagged behind in a quagmire of fear. The walls were a moldy gray, riddled with holes, sealed lockers, and rust-red handprints, while the wooden floor moaned with each step.

Worst of all was the silence, looming over them like a grim specter.

When they came to the art room in the east hall, Thaddeus's electro-staff shone on paper crafts and drawings. A draft came from a broken window and Victor shivered, eyes falling upon the stained tables and grisly doodles. One student, named Ingrid, had particularly vivid and disturbing works, all of doll-masked daemons.

Victor turned to Thaddeus. "How did this place become quarantined?"

"This was where the outbreak truly began, almost a year ago." Thaddeus shined the way forward. "The leprosy started in several of the slaughterhouses of Upton Meatpacking Company. A strain must have gotten into the pork. And when that very livestock proved to be tainted, it was already too late for Jericho District. We could not save those souls."

"Yeah," Leng elaborated. "The leprosy starts off benign, easily confused with melancholy. But in the final stages, you become rabid and ravenous, lashing out at anything and everything. Some people have another theory—that it's caused by the daemons."

"I see." Victor's eyes were glued to those drawings. "Horrible...."

Several doors down they came to the library, though

hardly a book was to be found. But he saw something in the shadows—a stuffed toy rabbit on a shelf. Odd. He used to have one exactly like it. And he reached for it, bombarded by memories of another time.

How long ago it seemed, back in the Waking World.

The fleeting spring of childhood, spent watching ducks drift in the townhouse's pond. It was a time of learning and joy, when Victor splashed monochromatic finger paints on an easel, but the moon slowly rose. Victor felt the anxiety that plagued all children to varying degrees. In hindsight, he suspected his talents were a shield against this primal fear.

The fear of growing up.

When Victor heard his mother's call he had always obeyed, taking a deep breath. He never slept easily, tossing and turning, but it came eventually as he nestled against his fifty-seven stuffed animals, sucking his thumb, eyes drifting shut, and—

"Victor," Thaddeus called, "We *must* continue."

"…yeah."

"It's just some one-eyed ragdoll." Leng furrowed his brow, coming to his side. "Who knows where it's been? I wouldn't touch it, to be honest." He paused. "Victor?"

"…yeah."

Victor picked the doll up, shoving it into his coat pocket. For some reason, the little thing comforted him. Leng gave him a disturbed look, but he cared not. And during a moment's rest, Victor, lost in thought, held the toy rabbit. This was all too strange, and yet, this was all something that he would have created, industrial yet fantastic. Hard as he tried to push such thoughts aside, they always came back, lingering as possibilities all too persistent.

"Why didn't y-you kill me?" he blurted.

Leng frowned. "Damn. That was curt."

"I'm just curious. I mean, the stormtroopers wanted me dead."

"I would be lying to say it's all law," Leng said. "Personally, I think you're not guilty of anything. You're an outsider, and too damn oblivious. But there's more than that. There *are* things I can't really explain, and I admit it. I mean, come on, you fell from the Iron Sky. Exactly what's happening, I can't really say."

Anything is possible at this point, I suppose....

As time dragged on, reality slowly warped and the windows shrank into the distance. Victor trailed after Thaddeus and Leng until the darkness grew into something hellish. The walls thickened with decay, and splotches of ichor dotted the ground. The ambiance was like blades screeching on steel drums, but he endured. And when they came to the courtyard, Victor saw only broken remnants of childhood—a playground looming over a field of barren concrete.

His heart plummeted to forlorn depths.

Surrounded by a gap-toothed picket fence, it was a multi-level structure of wooden platforms, built like a whimsical church. It was long since forsaken, paint chipped and sandboxes overgrown, braced with lattice works and decayed frames, swings swaying without wind, slides stained scarlet with rust. Doll heads dangled from the railings, and propped against its "steeple" was a dead television, a window into another world, and—

"Jesus fuck!" he blurted.

Not far away, Victor saw several corpses impaled on a telephone pole, those doll masks stitched to their faces, limbs rigid and wide like a tree of the dead. And yet not a single drop of blood was to be found. They were covered in puncture wounds, as if their fluids had been harvested by some vampiric killer.

"What?" Thaddeus seethed. "Will these murders never cease?!"

Leaning against the wall, Victor picked up the pieces of his shattered courage. Then he saw a pale envelope tacked on the black pole, with the name Victor Roland scribbled on it.

Thaddeus snatched the letter, handing it to him. "Open it."

"Wait," Leng objected. "Shouldn't we take it to forensics first?"

Thaddeus shot him a glare. With trembling hands, Victor opened the wax seal and read the typewritten contents aloud.

Dear Victor,

I am pleased that you managed to get this far. Welcome to Holy Gothica, a black hole filled with blood, shit, and diesel. I hope you enjoy your stay, and that my friends didn't treat you too harshly. But you've no doubt witnessed my work. I hope you find it as amusing as I do. I keep hearing rumors that the Inquisition has caught me, but they haven't just yet. I laugh to myself when they talk about being on "the right track." But the real joke is how I'm managing to get away with all this. This reaping will produce a bountiful harvest when I am done. Follow the breadcrumbs if you want answers. There are plenty to find, I assure you, for a new dawn is coming.

Good luck,
The Dollmaker

Leng stared over Victor's shoulder. "Well. That's disturbing—"

At that moment, a siren of white noise erupted from the tower.

"Run, Victor." Thaddeus drew his sword, grounding his staff. "Get to higher ground."

He obeyed, unquestioning, climbing a ladder to the top

of the play structure and staring upward, braced himself for the unknown. Victor watched the television flash on as a black hole of evil swirlings. Thaddeus's eyes narrowed. Another call blared from the radio tower and Leng winced, covering a bleeding ear and pointing a shaky revolver.

The first of many battles was about to begin.

#

As he leaned on the playground's railing, Victor's mind was wracked by the claws of discord. Thaddeus and Leng stared on, rooted by fleeting valor. For as doll masks bubbled up from the black miasma of the screens, their daemons apparated with abstract shapes.

Victor tried to scream, but his voice was siphoned away by shock.

They were the same things that had dragged him here—things of metal and wheels, covered in oil and ooze. Then the slithering slimes rose as spheres of blackness, twisting and writhing, taking the forms of gray children and teddy bears, as imps of the nameless hells.

They were perversions of youth. Their mumbles and whimpers reverberated in Victor's mind. Not only were these ghosts of children, but echoes of his own memories.

Bullies.... Threats.... Fear....

Some had crisscrossed slits or gaping holes for faces. Others wore masks of cracked china, with hollow pits of eyes and mouths of broken glass. They shivered, as animatronics draped in the skins of goblin-kids and taxidermies. Arms ending in hypodermic claws, one's jaw dropped. It let loose an all too human scream, and Victor knew they were puppets of evil.

"Go back to the hell that unchained you!" Thaddeus roared.

Leng slumped to his knees, trembling, and the daemons lunged, tackling Thaddeus with rasping screeches, slamming him against a pole. He collapsed, and they pinned him down with claws and shivs. From his hiding place Victor stared in terror, watching as Leng's eyes rolled back, wracked with convulsions, as the daemons ignored him and passed him by.

Then, one reared its head towards the playground tower, staring at Victor without eyes.

He leaned on the platform's edge until it gave way and he tumbled downward with a clatter. His deck of tarot cards scattered across the pavement and the daemons shrieked, as if blinded by the arcane images, and at that moment, Victor heard the whispers of the Opera House.

Go forth and fear not, for I am by your side, closer than you think.

Head throbbing and hands shaking, Victor felt the Music of the Spheres in his skull and time slowed once more, warped by the will of dreams. He felt the toy rabbit in his hand. Terrified, he listened as the daemons sang a "medley," nursery-rhymes distorted by chaos.

Is this how it ends?

The passing seconds seemed to last a lifetime. Victor could run away, leave his captors to die. After all, what would happen if he saved the inquisitors? He'd be taken to whoever ruled over this metropolis and be executed by a firing squad, if he were lucky.

"Victor." Thaddeus's voice buzzed with panic. "What are you doing?!"

At that moment, images flashed in his mind. Charles. Beatrice. Were they still out there? Were they even alive? He hadn't the faintest idea, but Victor could not find them alone. Something else kept him rooted — a sense of determination not easily quelled.

Although timid, he was no coward.

As the daemons crawled forward, Victor felt something

surge through him, thinking he was about to vomit until his mind cleared. His heart was a metronome and his thoughts played in tune. When Victor outstretched his hand, the cards rushed to his side. They orbited his wrists and head as halos of divination, choosing the lost boy as their rightful master.

How this happened, Victor did not know, nor did he care.

By the power of the cards, cobalt flames wrapped around the rabbit. A piece of his soul echoed beyond the flesh, manifesting through that simple toy. Ablaze, the rabbit floated ever upward until it erupted altogether, summoning a phantasm of Victor's own image.

From the very moment of my emergence, I have been watching over you as you slept, keeping the monsters of the mind at bay, a token of mother's love and the will to live. But as you matured, I took on another form. I came through the dark woods of error, through inferno and paradise alike, to guide you once more, as I did so many moons ago. I am Dante Alighieri, the Poet of the Spheres. I was always within you, and now, we are one.

For I am your Animi Firmatis.

Materializing above Victor was the truest reflection of his soul, buzzing in and out of existence as it enlarged and took form, an imaginary friend that also had grown up.

At least eight feet tall, its rabbit ears were long and drooping, its face a Venetian mask of music notes, a sole marble eye unblinking, fixed with a single purpose—to protect. And yet, it had a modern bent, cowl and crimson robes flowing like a Florentine trench coat. It clutched a grimoire of divine comedy, and a halberd blade curved as the crescent moon. And as its flames died, Dante's boots slammed down to Earth, booming against the shrieks and screams.

"W-what?" Thaddeus stammered in awe. "What *is* this miracle?"

Embracing his metamorphosis, Victor felt as if body and mind were one and the same. By the power within, Dante thrust its blade, impaling a leaping imp, watching as it burst into smoke and tar while the others quivered in dread.

Victor gave a mad grimace, awakening to a power most psychotic.

He jerked his hand forward and the eldritch poet dove into the darkness as the daemons sprung forth by the dozen. Dante's every swing was true, cleaving his foes asunder. Then two more lunged from the shadows, tackling the poet, clinging to it like starved leeches. Victor felt their glass teeth dig into his very soul as his bond with the summoning intensified.

"Get off me!" they screamed in harmony.

Cradling his skull, a surge of symphonic will coursed from Victor's mind as Dante pried the daemons off, stomping them into the concrete. But another lunged with a wretched shriek, slamming into him. Even as Victor skidded across the blacktop they loomed, claws outstretched. He felt as he had in the first nightmare, besieged by the nothingness lurking in his mind — the crushing solitude he so feared — but his determination did not falter.

"Dante!" he yelled. "Burn them by our holy flames!"

The summoned one outstretched an open hand, as if channeling the Symphonia Mundi itself, launching a bolt of divine fire, strumming like a cello. The daemons all lit up like dry pyres and wailed, shambling back. Victor staggered up, and when Dante sliced them all in a single cleaving motion, the flames died, and then....

A distant church bell filled the air.

Thaddeus staggered up, watching as the evil of the Devil's Hour crept back into the void, the dull world of men returning. In its wake the daemons dissolved, like dead skin flaking off charred corpses, leaving only ash and smoke. Consumed by this trance, Victor stared on as Dante turned to face the Iron Sky, converging back into that toy rabbit, the cards raining like confetti to the ground. Victor collapsed to his knees, the glow in his eyes dulling to normality.

Then, the world faded to an aria of white noise.

#

"Victor," a familiar voice echoed, mechanical yet human. "Victor Roland!"

Victor's eyes jerked open to see Thaddeus and Leng looming over him. The serfdoms were normal again—at least, as normal as Holy Gothica could be. Dazed by the gaslights, Victor was shaky and weak. He threw an arm over Thaddeus's shoulder and felt the inquisitor hoist him up.

"A-are you okay?" Victor wheezed. "Y-you're not hurt?"

"We're doing better than you," Leng said. "You were out cold."

Victor cradled his forehead, trying not to vomit. "I'm all right."

Thaddeus's eyes glistened with concern. "I am glad. The Cacophony besieges the senses of those unacquainted with its discordant power." He stared at the singed cards. "On another note, do you have any idea what you just did? What you awakened to?"

Victor did not reply. His head spun, consciousness fading in and out.

"You are not like us," Thaddeus said. "You are linked to the Symphonia Mundi, and absurdly so, might I add. Using the Imperial Tarot to summon a geist."

Victor stared onward, perplexed and disturbed. "What the hell is a geist?"

"Beings of inner power," Leng said, eyes fixed on the toy

rabbit. "Geists are mirrors of our minds. They take on different sides of our souls, facets of our psyches, links between ego and aether. About that Dante, though. Is he from your world?"

"Yes and no," Victor managed, regaining his strength. "A great poet of Florence, who wrote an epic famed in history. In it, he traversed Hell itself, guided by unrequited love." He gave a sad smile. "I first read his work in the ninth grade. But what does, 'Animi Firmatis,' mean?"

"It is an old phrase meaning the strength of the mind," Thaddeus said. "But you said that you had a reading before all this. That you drew the Moon Arcana, the omen of illusion and fantasy." He picked up that particular card. "Most intriguing."

Victor took the card and shoved it into the deck.

Thaddeus's eyes glistened with a warm respect. "Each arcana of the Imperial Tarot symbolizes an aspect or step in the journey of our lives, carrying us along the path from cradle to grave. These cards apply to all men, some deeper than others."

"W-what?" Victor didn't quite understand. "They're evoked by the cards?"

"Indeed," Thaddeus said. "Geists are not exempt from such rulings. They abide by the arcana even more than we. They are our reflections within the Symphonia Mundi, their celestial hierarchy parallel to the tarot itself. In the hands of a rare few, touched by the Music of the Spheres, this divine imagery can evoke a geist, binding it to one's soul as a guardian entity."

"So, they're psychological angels?" Victor asked. "That's fascinating."

"Be that as it may," Thaddeus turned to the carnage, "those were daemons, and I doubt we have seen the last of them. Some of my colleagues believe they are the Grand Conductor punishing us. For this many have lost faith, turning to darkness for comfort. The result is our regime of bitter necessity."

Victor looked away. "T-that's what those were? Good God."

Leng started at the broken television. "The Thirteenth Frequency alters the fabric of reality—it allows the daemons to breach the otherworld. Televisions and radios are the most common mediums, given their ties to the Symphonia Mundi and whatnot." He looked away. "I bet you this killer is using these tools as a kind of a weapon. Portals to Hell."

"Why are you telling me this?" Victor asked. "Isn't this all classified?"

"Perhaps I was wrong about many things." Thaddeus shuddered, as if saying that was painful. He held a trinket to the bodies impaled on the wires, eyes wide with horror. They were fetid and reeking, long left dangling here. Meanwhile, Victor noticed torn fishnets and corsets scattered about as soiled rags. Like all the others, they were women of the street.

"These victims also were drained of their vitae." Thaddeus withdrew a cotton swab and a vial of holy water. "It is a divine substance, the liquid residue of the soul, secreted from blood during times of great stress—such as torture and murder."

"Latent, it makes us sentient. But when it's active...." Leng's eyes widened, and he changed the subject. "Wait, Thaddeus, you don't mean—"

"I fear so." He watched the sample turn black. "This is a dark harvest of our very souls. And that letter from Hell only supports my claims." He looked Victor dead in the eye. "However, we are servants of order, and our mercy was returned in kind. You saved our lives."

Victor looked away, flattered. "I wouldn't go that far."

"You could have deserted," Leng smiled, "and had every reason to."

"Indeed, you have a noble heart, Victor," Thaddeus said.

"When one saves another's life here, that is something most sacred."

"But what do we do now? Are we still going to that Apostolic Palace?"

"Not to put you on trial," Thaddeus said. "As an inquisitor, I am the law. You are separated from your friends, that much I know. But first, we must solve yet another mystery—what exactly you are. Leng and I will do what we can, as there is much at stake, for all of us."

"You're both generous, but—" Victor sighed. "Fine, lead the way."

CHAPTER SIX

The fog had lifted for now. The inquisitors assured Victor the worst was over, though he found that hard to believe. In the inner-city neighborhoods, the acrid stench of coal was overwhelming — Industrial District was dominated by great factories, smokestacks jutting to the Iron Sky, their shanties populated only by the truly destitute. Victor barely noticed these beggars anymore. After the Leper Quarter, their company seemed pleasant by comparison.

"Disturbing." Leng broke the silence, his yellow raincoat like a caution sign against the urban decay. "I mean, who the hell writes a letter like that?"

"Who the hell butchers people and impales them on telephone poles?" Victor replied, shuddering. "That's a better question. Also, what's with the TVs?"

"Insanity is no rarity in our city," Thaddeus said. "Whoever this 'Dollmaker' is, I suspect he is aligned with the daemons, perhaps even using them as proxies for his vile plots. The Thirteenth Frequency allows such evil to possess some of our technologies — radios and televisions — as rifts. Those are powered by cymatic programs, and when those programs are corrupted...." He gave a low hiss. "Truly, we are dealing with a madman."

Leng frowned. "I remember a time when criminals had guilds and believed in something. Whoever this psychopath is, I don't think it's a coincidence he's targeting hookers."

"Nor I," Thaddeus said. "Still, we may want to obtain a warrant to Yoshiwara, again."

Leng snorted. "The red-light district? I know what you're thinking, but please, your lovers' quarrel theory was already debunked. Whoever's behind all this is clearly a thrill junkie."

"Our strongest leads are still those chocolatiers," Thaddeus said. "Edgar and Brutus."

Leng raised an eyebrow. "Wait, the Munchausen Brothers? Seriously?"

Those names sparked a memory in Victor's mind—the candyman from his arrival in this city, and that demented leper who'd pinned him against a wall. He had almost forgotten them.

How do they fit into all this?

Leng snorted. "Please, being a little weird doesn't make you a serial killer. Besides, Edgar's been locked up in the candy-making business, especially since Lady Fukuhara turned up dead." He looked away. "I'd know that better than most."

Then, Victor heard a jingle in the distance, a hurdy-gurdy over a loudspeaker.

"Speak of the devil," Thaddeus growled, laying a hand over the hilt of his sword.

"Goodies and chewies," a nasally voice said. "All for those young at heart!"

Victor turned his head, seeing that garish caravan rolling towards them, bells ringing along the cobblestone road, pulled by its automated stallion. Street urchins crawled from the alleys and shacks, turning their heads, eyes widening with excitement and joy.

"Come, little kiddies," Edgar called. "Poor? Penniless? We care not. All treats and tarts are *free* on the Sabbath!" Children chased after the truck as he tossed candy bars and lollipops out its windows, while his leprous brother, Brutus, drove on, his jawless face covered by a wooden mask, wheezing to himself. "Come," Edgar repeated, "we have plenty to spare."

What am I even looking at?

Victor couldn't help but smile. It was disturbing yet heartwarming, seeing the Munchausen Brothers at work. It reminded him of the Halloweens of his youth—a favorite holiday, free of yuletide anxieties. Like trick-or-treaters, the children were overjoyed, cheering in thanks, as if Edgar was some kind of angelic gift-bearer.

His top hat was punctuated by a peacock feather, and his suit was stained silver and orange—a gentleman clown, putting on a happy face for these "kiddie-widdie-winkies."

"He is certainly an odd fellow," Thaddeus said.

"Not gonna deny that." Leng crossed his arms. "But the man has a heart of gold." His eyes followed the children, faces beaming past soot and filth. "Can't name anyone else quite like him. Who gives two shits about these bastards? That said, he's a little naive."

"What's his story?" Victor asked. "Why do you even suspect him?"

"He is a friend to all children," Thaddeus said. "But that is only a part of who he is. Leng might be more apt at explaining this."

The wagon came to a slowing halt.

"And what would *you* like?" Edgar leered from the open window, asking a little girl in a burlap dress. "I have feta tarts, saltwater taffy, lemon bars...."

Leng shook his head as if in pity. "He fell head over heels with this courtesan. Never go after a woman who sells herself. Because we all know how Fukuhara wound up—impaled on a telephone pole. And she wasn't the last. Since that night, we've had a serial murder case."

Victor raised an eyebrow. "Sounds like you know him well."

Leng sighed deeply. "What happens in Yoshiwara *stays* there. Trust me, kid. Between 'fondue on the nip' and...." He chuckled, as if reliving a rather vivid exploit. "Anyway, Edgar and I, we knew each other. We pregamed at Hatter's a lot, climbing the ladder, and then—"

"Climbing the ladder?" Victor asked.

"A colloquialism. It refers to the use of a particular stimulant," Thaddeus explained, "Ladder is a controlled substance, commonly used among the homeless and harlots."

"Heh," Leng smirked. "You're the only one who can make getting high sound boring, Thaddeus. But you're missing my point. Even if Edgar frequents Yoshiwara, so do a lot of people. Even me. And last I checked, my record's clean."

As the inquisitors went further off topic, Victor noticed the girl's ragdoll—a love worn thing, with a head of broken china. He shuddered, remembering those daemons not an hour ago.

It has to be a coincidence....

"Something just doesn't sit right with him," Thaddeus said. "Remember, Edgar's toys bear an uncanny resemblance to those masks. The ones found on the victims."

Leng sighed. "So? Those puppets are kind of generic. I've seen many like them." He glanced at the malformed driver. "And if you're thinking of his brother, Brutus is far more creepy than dangerous. That circus freak's a real simpleton. Too clumsy to pull off these stunts. I highly doubt either of them know how to work the radios like that."

Then, Victor felt Edgar's gaze turning to them.

"Salutations, grim ones." He waved, like a celebrity on parade. "Are we too old to join the fun? Is there no rest for the Inquisition? Such a demanding job. Have you been good?" He grinned mockingly. "Not too many executions, I hope. Here, here." He tossed a handful of candy at their feet — Victor caught a pack of "fantasy sour belts." He'd always liked those.

Leng didn't look at the chocolatier. "Still coping, huh?"

"Why go through life dull and gray?" Edgar leaned his chin on a fist, a dreamy mania in his eyes. "I simply choose to spread my joy to those in need. At any rate," his smile turned hollow, "you mustn't talk about someone who's listening. You don't want to set a bad example for the wee ones, do you?"

Victor took a step back, more than a little embarrassed. Thaddeus's eyes narrowed, but he said nothing. With that, Edgar and Brutus wished the children farewell as the automated stallion pulled the carriage into the darkening slums, its chimes fading into the distance.

"If not Edgar," Thaddeus said, "who do you suspect, Leng?"

"Want my opinion? Bet you it's that industrialist, Doctor Murdoch."

"Murdoch? That man is dead," Thaddeus hissed. "Dead, and you know it."

"W-who's Murdoch?" Victor looked between them. "H-hey!"

"No corpse." Leng shoved his hands into his pockets. "No word for a good year, either. After that censored project he went psycho. Got excommunicated for heretical ravings. Then, the *really* weird shit started happening. It's only getting worse with murder thrown into the mix. And he was last seen in the Leper Quarter, where all this began. I mean, who wouldn't be pissed, if your state turned against you overnight like that?"

Thaddeus shook his head. "I highly doubt this."

"I know you two were friends. But I still think you're in—"

Thaddeus's eyes twitched with wrath. "Shut up."

Leng took a step back. "Whoa. No need to get angry."

Thaddeus did not reply, marching and leading the way far ahead, silently seething. Leng and Victor lagged behind, not wanting to test him further. Left to his own devices, Victor tasted the rainbow candies—they were far more tart than he remembered.

CHAPTER SEVEN

An hour later, Victor and the inquisitors crossed into Serfdom One, and the Informatorium Square. Here, built into the gargantuan supports of the Phonos Engine, Victor saw something rising amongst the libraries and dull apartments—a church of concrete and tubes, typewriters singing like the choir of bureaucracy from within, its brass placard reading,

CENTRAL SERVITORIUM

"How do we get to the Apostolic Palace?" Victor called. "I'm confused."

"The Great Lifts of the Phonos Engine are giant elevators," Leng explained. "We can use them to get from the Serfdoms to the City Above in just a few minutes. Cool, huh?"

"Also," Victor realized something else, "just how many people know about those surges? That—Devil's Hour. And wouldn't those daemons ravage the entire city during them?"

"It is the Inquisition's duty to maintain a 'masquerade' of sorts," Thaddeus said. "There is no official statement or acknowledgment regarding the Thirteenth Frequency. To admit such a phenomenon would send the populace into a rioting panic." He turned to a few thuggish passersby. "Power failures and drug-dealing gangers provide our — "

"Scapegoats?" Victor raised an eyebrow.

"Anyway." Leng shrugged. "When people turn into statues, it's kind of hard to notice what's going on. Let alone prove anything. Besides, the daemons just lurk and feed off the psyches of the masses. They don't even touch the people. I mean, it might have something to do with our depression rate skyrocketing, but that's about it."

"Oh, yeah," Victor muttered. "Totalitarianism has *nothing* to do with that."

"Regardless," Thaddeus said, "we must get permission from the curators to reach the City Above, let alone the Apostolic Palace. All roads in the serfdoms lead to their analytical engines, running the city's administrative and mechanical functions."

The doors swung open, and Victor's boots clomped down a long marble hall. The inquisitors were silent, and he thought it best to act the same.

Beneath a ceiling of arches and gilded ducts, a burgundy carpet divided this hall in two. On either side were the various departments of Holy Gothica, filled with cubicles and oaken desks, alive with the tapping of keyboards and cogitators, reeking of fresh ink and stale cigarettes. It was a monastery of paperwork, with monks in suits and ties, and its nave ended at a waiting room, where a number of motley serfs sat in prayer, watched over by an altar of administration. And there, a curator reviewed all manner of texts with bitter studiousness.

"Damn," Leng hissed. "He still works here?"

Thaddeus's brow furrowed. "Who are you blathering about now?"

"My old boss, Brendel." Leng shoved his hands deep into his pockets. "That bastard has his head so far up his ass, he's a living colonoscopy. Thought he died of leprosy."

Sitting behind a tall, oaken desk, the old man's face was weathered and lean, eyes magnified by thick glasses. His ink-stained fingers slammed away at a typewriter as a massive screen loomed overhead, displaying a list of two-bit numerals.

"I'll handle him," Leng carried on. "After all, I am an inquisitor now."

"Leng," Thaddeus warned, "don't do anything rash. And do not mention Victor's...abilities. I want to keep that as unspoken as possible."

"Calm your metal tits, Thaddeus. I got this covered."

Victor decided to sit by the pews, watching with morbid curiosity, while Thaddeus stood not far away, as if bracing himself for a storm of mortification. As they waited, Victor noticed a stack of fliers and forms with a gossip journal to the side, with the title, *"WHO IS REALLY BEHIND THE DOLLMAKER MURDERS?!"* in crimson font. Victor couldn't help but smirk at the sensationalism, and skimmed a page.

This week marks the third reported killing committed by the Dollmaker, who stalks the red-light district of Yoshiwara, leaving a trail of blood in his wake. The first and only identifiable victim was Lady Himiko Fukuhara, the proprietor of the Sunset Pagoda, who had a torrid love affair with one of her "guests," Edgar Munchausen. Although a known industrialist and chocolatier, one must raise the question: is he really "a friend to all those young at heart," or does he moonlight as a lust-driven serial killer?

"Please," a familiar voice cried. "I paid your form-tithes. I need to reach the Apothecary! What else do you want? What can I do?"

Victor raised his head. At the end of the desk stood a familiar leper, pleading before the podium. A pair of stormtroopers fiddled with their rifles to keep her at bay, and Victor realized this was the leper from the Cathedral Ward.

"Due to an update in our system," Brendel replied without inflection, "I cannot accept these particular papers at this time—as of last week, actually. I recommend you visit the administrators, and contract them for the new, proper forms, and—"

"I filled this out two weeks ago, and you wouldn't accept it!" the leper shouted. "You said the systems were being updated! What else am I supposed to do? Just rot in the slums until I die? I've done nothing wrong! I am a human being, dammit!"

Victor took a few steps forward, but the stormtroopers pointed their rifles and unlocked their safeties, preparing to open fire.

"Moreover, according to this medical form," Brendel said, straightening his glasses, "you tested positive for the later stages of leprosy."

"What...?"

"You display enough symptoms, courtesy of your blood sample, to be considered truly contagious and therefore a threat to our society." Brendel laid a handkerchief to his mouth. "Take her to the Leper Quarter, and update her records to ensure she remains in that ghetto." He cleared his throat. "Number 1138, step forward."

"No!" The leper screamed, but the stormtroopers grabbed her biceps with thick gloves and dragged her back down the hall. "You can't do this! You inhumane bastard! I'll—"

A stormtrooper cracked a baton against the leper's spine, silencing her. Many thoughts raced through Victor's mind. Were these people conditioned to accept horror? Was human nature really so malleable as to allow this brutal society? Or was it simply the hegemonic elite extorting the populace?

Regardless, dystopia was not easily maintained. Though the impracticality of the system was apparent, it too was a body of oppression, and—

"Number 1138," Brendel repeated. "Step forward."

Another pasty serf stood up, legs aquiver, but Leng flashed his badge and marched forward, clearing his throat loudly.

"Papers." Brendel did not lift his nose from his bookkeeping. "If you require the standard documentation to access the City Above, please refer to the administrators. They can assist you with the proper forms, and—"

"That won't be necessary," Leng replied, standing tall.

"Oh?" Brendel raised an eyebrow. "Oh...Walter. I thought the Inquisition took you away. Have you a code clearance?"

"Better." Leng placed his iron rosette on the desk. "It's Ser Walter Leng of Her Holiness's Inquisition now. We require access to the Great Lifts, if you please."

Thaddeus laid a palm to his face, but said nothing.

Brendel smirked. "An inquisitor? Never would have thought. But may I ask your business? Even inquisitors must obey Ecclesiastical protocol. I trust you understand." His voice dripped with sarcasm. "You above all should know the protocols of our church-state, Walter."

"*Ser* Walter Leng."

"Whatever," Brendel muttered. "Pretentious as ever."

"Anyway, our business is our own." Leng shot Thaddeus a wink. "It is a delicate matter that must be kept discreet. I trust you understand." He leaned on the desk. "Remember the Fourth Textile Fire? How we had to make *that* discreet too? Similar principles."

"Please, don't talk about historical revision in front of the serfs." Brendel gritted his wooden dentures. "You can't talk your way out of an answer. You should know that by now."

"Come on, state security trumps red tape. Everyone knows that."

Thaddeus watched in embarrassment until the inquisitor stood, muttering something about "proper forums" before marching to another service desk. Meanwhile, Victor had to keep himself from laughing at the absurdity of it all. But every time Leng's voice rose, he lowered it at once, as if he retained a hint of respect for the Servitorium—until his store of patience ran thin.

"Oh, for fuck's sake," Leng said, rolling his eyes. "Just get us on the elevator."

"I'm afraid I can't let you board."

"Why not?"

"I reserve the right to question your character." Brendel pushed the iron rosette back. "How do I know this is an authentic badge of the Inquisition? You don't exactly have a clean record when it comes to forgery. We both remember *that* incident."

"Never going to let me live that down, are you?"

"Why should I? Corrections don't lie, unlike your penmanship."

"Enough." Thaddeus returned with a cardstock folder. "Your pardon, but I am Ser Hector Thaddeus, and I assure you, while Leng is an insufferable fool, he does not lie at this time. Our purpose is as delicate as it is urgent." He slid a few papers over with his own iron rosette. "I have the supplementary forms for transportation as well, should you require them."

"Very well." Brendel took his time, reading the fine print and signatures with unrelenting care, and when he stamped the passport section, he sighed, "You have no record of forgery, but I wish you had interrupted your idiot colleague earlier." He slid the rosette and papers back, handing Thaddeus a copper keycard. "Lift two is the second door, after two lefts and a right. But Leng," he called after them, "*never* return to my office."

Leng said nothing, gritting his teeth. Victor thought it best not to say anything. As the three strode down the hall, the stormtroopers before the leftmost entrance stepped aside. Its corridor was a piece of the Phonos Engine's bowels, and despite iron walls a foot thick, Victor heard the Music of the Spheres, warping into a monkish chant of metal and wheels.

"Consider the Phonos Engine a massive processing cogitator," Thaddeus explained. "It is truly a wonder of the world. It distills the power transferred from the Azoth reactors around the city perimeter, making its cymatic energy useable and distributing it throughout the Serfdoms." He stood before the gilded doors of lift two. "It draws from the Symphonia Mundi itself in subtle ways, while being directly powered by Azoth."

"Yeah," Leng added. "Azoth is the mineral residue of the Symphonia Mundi, very powerful, but very radioactive. So, we have to be careful when using it, to avoid meltdowns." He cringed. "That's never fun to deal with—for anyone."

Victor cocked his head. "Like nuclear fission?"

Thaddeus nodded. "You understand more than you let on. Far more than I guess."

Above the doors to the Great Lifts, Victor saw the words on its placard, shining like a sacred scripture. At first he expected them to hold some enlightened meaning, until he read them, recognizing the phrase all too well.

MEMENTO MORI

"Do you know what that means?" Thaddeus asked.

"Remember your death?" Victor felt a shiver down his spine. "An old phrase."

"It is our creed and motto," Thaddeus said. "Death is what

makes us men. A testament to our common fate. Lord or serf, none can escape it. But death is also a path to something else, a place where no wish lies unfulfilled. For light is the bliss of blinding nothingness. *Lux Ex Oblivione*." He pushed open the elevator doors. "Come, now." When they boarded, he pressed a brass button and the lift trembled, taking flight. "Before us lay the Vaults of Prayer."

#

Gothic windows lined the Great Lifts, facing the serfdoms in full. As the minutes dragged on, Victor stared from the escalating heights and saw just how vast the downtrodden districts were. But the greatest sights of all came from within the Phonos Engine itself. It was a dim tower, covered with massive engines like the inner workings of a clock tower, lined with stained glass, chrome lathes, and cobalt lights.

But it was far from silent.

Humming with echoing pianos and distant chimes, the radiance was swallowed by the enveloping darkness. For though such lights burned ever on, it was a cold, hollow place. And Victor saw thousands of little engines along the walls, their flames dancing in tune to these swan-songs, marked with placards of countless numbers.

And then, Victor heard sourceless voices of confession.

"Come, O' Far Messiah, be our guest. And let these gifts of salvation to us be blest. Let us be ever mindful of the Grand Conductor's continuous care, and let us be drawn closer to You."

Victor's eyes widened, as he realized just what these were. *An archive of confessions?*

"Any particular reason you are staring?" Thaddeus asked. "It is all right, you can talk."

"Huh?" Victor glanced away, a tad embarrassed. "I-it's

80

nothing."

"There is no need to lie. What's on your mind?" Thaddeus asked. "You have seen the confessionals in the slums, no? The automated sermons and mass?" He nodded. "It is a hard thing to miss. An oddity, I do admit. However, our state is not a sham, Victor. And the Phonos Engine and its vaults are a testament to this."

Victor was mesmerized by this place. "This is like a library of souls."

"Kinda," Leng said, "When every sermon ends, all the faithful enter those booths, confessing and praying, giving a blood sample. Their words are archived here, as requiems for dreams, I guess. But the samples are processed into vitae—you know, to give the words meaning. It's like an archive of hope, where we survey its records."

"Indeed," Thaddeus interjected. "These thoughts, tied to crystals of the bloodborne soul, are as seed cases against the wind of the Symphonia Mundi. Their words are recorded on the radios, and the radios are tied to the Music of the Spheres. Together, they are contained and catalogued in miniature consoles, sustaining their merit in a timeless form."

"Why though?" Victor asked. "Why release words into— whatever this is?"

"So they may last forever." Thaddeus bowed his head. "All fear death, but here, in the Vaults of Prayer, a piece of one's self is kept as a keepsake and a tombstone. A testament to one's fleeting life. It is a small comfort, yes, but it has its uses. Confessions of true heresy are met with merciful penance after their trial, as opposed to a summary execution."

A long silence passed as Victor listened to the wishes of the masses

"I pray for the strength to leave my life of carnal sin."

"I pray that I may find a place to call home."

"I pray to, one day, see the sun with my sister."

Victor heard many more from throughout the city's history, flooding his mind with sorrow. "Spying on the confessors?" He gritted his teeth. "That's *horrible*. What do you do with the good thoughts? Lock and hoard them, like trophies?"

"You assume far too much," Thaddeus growled. "The Sect of Charity takes the broken dreams of the downtrodden. They attempt to repair them within the boundaries of the law. For all nations, even ones as draconian as mine, are not without good men."

Victor's heart sank. He said nothing.

"There is something else, though."

"Well, I mean...." Victor tried to articulate his thoughts. "I've never met an officer so...."

"Maverick?"

"Yeah, what's your story? How did you become an inquisitor?"

"There is a time for everything, but that is not now. Nor am I not supposed to speak of it. What about you, Victor? You mentioned another world on many occasions."

Victor gave the inquisitor a cockeyed look. "Is this another planet?"

Thaddeus shook his head. "I have heard of a realm beyond the confines of this material plane; perhaps you may call it, 'home.' Regardless, it is where the Far Messiah originated." His brow furrowed. "An odd coincidence, no?"

Victor did not reply, beginning to understand this world. Many minutes passed, but when the elevator docked with a locking clunk, far above the earthly slums, he saw the night sky again.

"Welcome to the City Above," Leng announced. "Safest

place in all the Imperium."

CHAPTER EIGHT

Disembarking, Victor stared in awe at this summited city, while Thaddeus and Leng stood just behind, unfazed. It was a chessboard of gothic apartments and government buildings, their bell towers and chimneys dominating the skyline. They were surpassed only by the cooling towers of Azoth reactors, belching smog into the late night air.

"Where are we?" Victor looked about. "Is this above the Iron Sky?"

"Indeed." Thaddeus took a few steps forward. "The City Above touches the heavens themselves as the highest office of the Ecclesiarchy, who administer the metropolis and our entire Third Gothic Imperium. And it is the duty of every man to keep such an order."

"How did your people create all this? I mean, it's beautiful, in a way, but—"

"There are many industrialists and inventors in Holy Gothica, all sanctioned by our Ecclesiarchy, but none were quite so great as Doctor Murdoch. He alone is responsible for such feats as the Phonos Engine. However, sickness of the mind befell him, among far darker things."

Darker things?

Though the layout of The City Above was aligned with the serfdoms below, it was a far cry from those impoverished ghettos. Further ahead, brilliant lights hung from parapet to parapet, and colorful banners draped the walls. Preparations for a new year's carnival were underway. Booths and tents lay under the turrets, where peddlers stocked their shelves with toys, trinkets, and tiny games. The refreshments included soda, ginger ale, and ice cream, perhaps "sanctioned substitutes" for the liquor below. Everyone here, be they dancer or clown, wore a mask, all dramatic and vibrant, gilding the City Above with bread and circuses.

"Ah," Thaddeus said. "I almost forget about this holiday."

"Interesting," Victor said. "What does it celebrate?"

"We are still preparing for the merrymaking, though soon, we will enjoy the Circus of Hours." Thaddeus gestured to the booths. "It is a yearly reminder of the passage of time, and for some the transition from youth to adulthood. We have games and festivities in celebration of our faith. Moreover, this year's carnival shall coincide with the coronation of our Holy Pontiff and Empress, who resides in the Apostolic Palace."

Thaddeus stopped, his eyes lifting ever upward, before that tremendous bastion. Its battlements were dotted with searchlights, gates braced with iron and marble. Like all Ecclesiastical buildings, the capitol was draped with monochromatic banners and topped with a clock tower, whose lights projected the state crucifix, gargoyles encircling its peak.

"It is the citadel of all men of faith." Thaddeus gazed in reverence and piety. "Our chiefest and greatest stronghold against the tides of darkness, whatever they may be."

Leng stared into the distance. "Well. I'd love to stay and chat," he said, "but I have to fill out the paperwork for forensics.

85

Especially after that little incident." He flipped the Dollmaker's letter in his fingers, turning to Thaddeus. "Take care of him, won't you?"

"I shall."

After Leng departed with a wave, Victor and Thaddeus walked down the street, towards the Apostolic Palace. But then Victor saw the moon shine out of the smog, far greater than the one of Earth, something out of an eerie impressionist painting. Its rays shone past the dark clouds, and Victor saw alien formations along its surface, like a grimacing face in the sky.

It's close, almost too close. This is not Earth.

"Come," Thaddeus said. "We must seek an audience with the Empress."

"That seems a little extreme," Victor said. "Isn't there some kind of—I don't know, Inquisitorial Council or something?"

"Yes," Thaddeus continued as they walked together, "but the Ordos are mostly autonomous. And the Inquisition as a whole is answerable to no one save the Empress herself. I shall tell her what I know of you, and leave the rest to her righteous judgment."

Victor shuddered. "What if that 'judgment's' not—?"

Thaddeus's eyes glistened in the moonlight. "Fear not, for I have faith that the Empress will be understanding of your plight, and willing to assist you however she can."

Somehow I doubt that.

Before Victor could speak, the Great Gates creaked open as Thaddeus raised his badge. Beyond lay a garden of unmatched beauty, filled with hedge mazes and cobbled walkways. At its center was a fountain, with an image of a man hoisting a flat world above his shoulders, water cascading from the disc's edges and pouring from his eyes like tears. But the closer Victor

looked, the more it resembled himself, its metal placard reading,
THE FAR MESSIAH

This harrowed him greatly, and he knew why.

The Royal Guard made way, all violet robes and iron arms, and they entered the palace's gothic halls. The walls were lined with tapestries of chivalric imagery, every curved window holding a view of the urban skyline and the arid wastelands beyond. Victor wanted to linger, but there was still a meeting to attend.

Finally they arrived at the war room where the clergy plotted their campaigns, though Victor could make nothing out save murmuring behind the door.

"Listen carefully," Thaddeus stated. "It is important that you show the utmost respect to our Holy Pontiff and Empress. Follow my lead and do not speak unless spoken to. Understood?"

Victor nodded and his guide opened the door.

#

Thaddeus and Victor beheld a domed chamber, where a council surrounded a table. They were a decadent lot, surreal in their excess, so detached from the destitution just beneath their feet. Their servants, a fusion of smooth flesh and silver castings, served the Ecclesiarchs cheese and tarts, while they debated over an atlas of Holy Gothica and its holdings.

"We have received reports that the rebels are regrouping in the Wastes, towards our very doorstep," one ambassador said, his commissar cap too small for his head. "Ever since the Powder Kegs first spread their dogma, civil unrest grows among the outlying fiefs. The people want more protection in exchange for their tithes."

"This is absurd!" A noblewoman spat, as the argent labori adjusted her powdered wig, spraying her with a puff of perfume. "Clearly the right to militia is protection enough. How much longer must we coddle our vassals? Increase the tithes and cut their power, I say."

"Agreed," said a dandy of ambiguous gender, leaning on a blackthorn cane. "But we should be cautious as to their strategic value. And while the long-term campaign should play itself out, one thing is clear—they are on the move. If these backwaters should fall under their control, the rebellion may well reach Holy Gothica proper."

The first commissar turned to a distant woman. "What say you, My Empress?"

Victor's eyes wandered, from general to garish bishop, until he saw just who the Empress really was. To think Victor had expected her to be a miserable nun with a fascist streak.

The Empress stood far from the bickering council, staring out an open window, gazing across the Ash Mountains. She was youthful, only a few years older than Victor, and at least six feet tall. Her garb was clerical yet regal, befitting a papess and queen, her hair flowing like rivulets of silver as the Lady of the Ecclesiarchy, and yet her eyes were as rubies, sharp and unrelenting.

Thaddeus knelt. "Hail, Holy Pontiff and Empress, Johanna d'Gothica. I come with—"

"Ser Hector Thaddeus." She did not look at him. "You must know I am most busy."

"I would not intrude unless the circumstances demanded it." Thaddeus rose on his own accord, to Johanna's slight disturbance. "You must listen to those you'd rather not."

The ambassadors exchanged nervous glances. Victor thought it best to retreat into social oblivion, as he often did with uncomfortable affairs. Most of the aristocrats averted their eyes from this "philistine," save the dandy, who gave Victor a flirty smile.

He almost didn't hear the conversation until Johanna spoke up.

"I will entertain your council, if it so pleases you," she said. "As I said, make it quick. In times such as these, I need to make my expectations clear to my subordinates."

"Your pardon, my lady," Thaddeus said. "I have found something that may help us during these dark times. When I was reassigned to accost this outsider, our machines detected a shift and rumination in the Music of the Spheres. I suspect it was an awakened power."

Johanna was still unreadable. "Go on."

As Thaddeus recounted their journey, Victor's mind wandered, listening to a waltz on the phonograph, trying to ignore the dandy's unrelenting gaze—until he noticed the Empress staring through him. She raised an eyebrow, and his stomach dropped.

"*This* is your weapon?" She scoffed. "I don't have time for this."

Victor stifled a flash of indignation, face turning scarlet.

"He is *the* outsider," Thaddeus raised his voice, just enough to get the Empress's attention. "Do not let his outlandishness fool you. I once thought as you do. Then I bore witness to his power. He has innate control over the Imperial Tarot and evoked a geist. I have never seen or read of its caliber, not even as transcribed in the Codex Gigas."

"A geist?" Johanna's interest was piqued, if only for a moment. "As in a summoner of old? Thaddeus, do you speak of the Far Messiah?"

Victor's embarrassment vanished, as he held back the words,

What the fuck…?

Thaddeus nodded. "He remains ignorant of our troubles, and Holy Gothica herself, for that matter. Regardless, I believe he is just that."

Victor was overcome by dizziness. He retreated to the sofa, laying his face in his hands, much to the dandy's amusement. The council sipped glasses of port, puckering their lips, watching this scandalous spectacle. A labori offered Victor a selection of liquors, but he declined with a wave. He would drink at a less pivotal time.

"You were right to interrupt." Johanna glanced at Victor again, but quickly looked away. "Forgive my harshness, but you must understand, I have enough affairs to cope with without talk of prophecy and fate." She gestured out the window. "This land was founded by men inspired by the heavenly works, and now it stands upon the brink of chaos. And yet, we know who is responsible for these late unpleasantries."

"I am afraid I do not follow," Thaddeus said. "Responsible?"

"We have reason to believe there is a *single* culprit behind these murders," the commissar said, his voice rife with poison. "Your peers in the Inquisition believe this as well."

"Moreover," Johanna continued, "We also have reason to believe Doctor Murdoch is the said culprit. Some say the Inquisition purged him in secret for his heretical ravings. I can testify this is not the case. He is alive, and I suspect his hatred has only worsened over time." Her gaze cut through Thaddeus. "You knew him once, did you not?"

Thaddeus looked away, eyes glistening with regret.

"He was my friend." He straightened. "But I was not present for his trial and sentence. I know the stormtroopers took everything upon his excommunication. I did not intend for them to do what they did. Burning his life's work, casting him into the Leper Quarter, like a criminal."

The ambassadors gave disapproving murmurs.

"Darkness warps the mind—you above all should know that, Inquisitor." Johanna's eyes narrowed. "This a matter of heresy. Do the Imperium proud and bring him to justice." She paused. "Have you anything else to say?"

"Indeed. What of the outsider?" Thaddeus asked.

"Let me clarify," she sighed. "I have no time for 'second comings' or 'gods in human form.' Not to mention, this superstitious tale occurred during the Thirteenth Frequency." She pursed her lips. "Surprisingly, the complete lack of evidence does not support your claims. I do not disbelieve you. However, I *am* troubled by your obsession with the esoteric."

Thaddeus drew a heavy breath; Victor could feel his rage brewing.

"Should you feel so inclined," Johanna said, "your ward is welcome to accompany you on your next assignments. Meanwhile, inquisitors of my own choosing will gather the most plausible leads, to assist you in empirical endeavors." She let that sink in. "The Imperium has come a long way since the barbarism of my forebears' reign. You would do well to modernize your methods if you wish to keep your position in my court."

"You know the law of the land." Thaddeus tried to mask the spite in his voice. "It was written long before your election by our clergy. Before the founding of the Imperium, even. In the event of the Far Messiah's descent, the Ecclesiarchy would—"

"Evidence." Johanna raised her voice. "Do not remind me of the Imperial Creed. Everything I do is for the good of the state. No matter how harsh it may seem." A bitter quiet passed, and she turned around. "Once I find a proper course of action, you will resume the investigation. With or without your prisoner."

First arrested, then interrogated, and now, Victor was press-ganged into prophecy. Even so, he knew these negotiations were over, as Thaddeus twitched with fettered wrath.

"Very well." The inquisitor seethed but obeyed. He and Victor departed down the long hall until out of earshot. "All has turned to vain ambition," Thaddeus hissed. "She has traded our piety for the decadence of empires."

#

Thaddeus and Victor came to a tower side balcony overlooking the metropolis, watching rays of starlight shine behind clouds of smog as the moon leered over all.

"I must find a way around this," Thaddeus said to himself. "I must control my anger."

Victor was lost in thought. He stared at the smoke-stacked skyline, trying to comprehend what had brought him here. Uncertainty gnawed at his mind, and more than anything else, he wanted to know what to do, if anything at all.

"I still do not understand," Victor said. "Far Messiah. What does that even mean?"

"If you believe in such things," Thaddeus said, as if reciting an epic poem, leaning on the railing. "The Far Messiah is, indirectly, the creator of the world and everything in it, for His dreams are not just dreams. He is the living incarnation of the Grand Conductor, and the geists are born of His divinity." He turned to Victor. "I saw what I saw, and one of the hallowed answered your call. This 'Dante' is a part of you. It is your alter ego in lucid dreams, a guardian angel evoked by the Imperial Tarot. This world is a far cry from your home, yet it is clear to me now why you are so bound to the Music of the Spheres. It is a rippled reflection of your thoughts and fantasies, underpinning the very city I call home. How you arrived I do not know, though one thing is clear to me — you *are* the Far Messiah."

"But why was I brought here? What must I do?"

"That I cannot tell you, for I do not know either." Thaddeus looked away. "Much of our faith was lost to the ages, and the Ecclesiarchy preaches only what remains, dictated by the will of the Holy Pontiff and Empress." He sighed, as if acknowledging the flaw in that.

Victor stared across the dark city. He remembered his humble beginnings, and they did not leave him. What had he really done but blindly accept this "destiny"?

All ignorance aside, he knew there was a long road ahead.

"Regardless," Thaddeus said. "Now that I have collected you, my orders are to continue investigating the Dollmaker Murders. I am an agent of the Inquisition, and it is my duty to fulfill that role. However, I have one more request." He turned to Victor, eyes glimmering. "One month has passed since I suspect your friends descended, and one month has passed since the first murder. These two events may be connected. I ask you to join me, unofficially, to—"

Charles, Beatrice…. If they were here, then Thaddeus could find them. Help was help, and like it or not, this was something that had to be done.

"If there's no other way," Victor interrupted, "I'll go with you."

Thaddeus lay a hand on his shoulder. "No one is forcing this upon you. Only join me if you truly will it. I do not know what will happen down there."

Victor stifled a shudder, feeling Thaddeus's metallic grip through his tattered coat, but he broke a soft smile. "If there's anyone I can rely on, it's you and Leng."

Thaddeus bowed his head. "I have reason to believe your friends are at Yoshiwara. Once the Holy Empress gathers her leads, we shall depart. It would be foolhardy to act before then. For now, I shall escort you to somewhere safe. Where we can both rest until the morrow."

"Very well," Victor said. "Thank you, Thaddeus."

"You are most welcome." Thaddeus stared at the night sky. "Odd, isn't it?"

"Hmm?" Victor didn't catch on. "What are you talking about?"

"Never before have I seen a moon quite of that size, looming over us like a black omen. Almost as if it could come crashing down at any moment."

Victor's stomach dropped. "C-crashing down?"

Thaddeus looked away. "Your pardon. I am merely talking to myself. The Hunter's Moon always marks the new year. At any rate, it has been a long day for us both."

As the inquisitor marched indoors, Victor glanced at the moon one last time.

"Yeah...you're right."

CHAPTER NINE

The Apostolic Palace faded into the distance, hardly a series of steeples on the horizon. Thaddeus led Victor through the curving suburbs along the city perimeter, in the shadow of baroque apartments yet safe under their gaslights. Beyond a thin stretch of greenbelt, by weeping willows and rose bushes, they came to a townhouse nestled between pastel boutiques. At first Victor thought they were headed to some covert facility, until Thaddeus sighed, rummaging for a set of house keys. Then, Victor saw the address.

1414 BOSCH STREET

Thaddeus opened the front door and flicked on a buzzing light.

"Welcome to my home," he said. "Please, make yourself comfortable."

Despite all sense, Victor felt at ease here. It was a neat and tidy place. The wallpaper was of a classical print, the walls themselves lined with bookshelves and oil paintings. An effigy of the Imperial Crest hung above the fireplace, while a reading chair was tucked by the window. A staircase lay at the hall's end, leading to some sort of cellar. The apartment smelled of soap and mint tea, more like a grandfather's house than any fascist headquarters.

Truth be told, Victor didn't know what to think.

Thaddeus put his trench coat and hat on a hook by the door, propping his thumbs under a pair of suspenders. "Help yourself to what I have in the icebox," he said. "There should be some tea biscuits, brie, and spiced jam. I was saving that, but you are my guest for tonight."

Victor's stomach growled. He hadn't eaten in over eight hours.

"Know what? I'll take it all," he said. "I haven't eaten since—"

Thaddeus's brow furrowed. "Pardon? The whole platter?"

Victor looked away, realizing he could probably eat the entire pantry.

Not the best etiquette.

"It is quite all right." Thaddeus opened the icebox, and a chill wafted through the air. "You need it more than I do." He gave a vibrating chuckle, handing Victor a full plate wrapped in plastic. "You are welcome to stay, while I go about the duller parts of the investigation."

Such implications did not dawn on Victor yet.

"Yeah." He slathered his tongue with bread and cheese, bombarded by different flavors and textures with each culinary combination. "Goddamn, this is really good."

Thaddeus raised an eyebrow.

"Uh." Victor raised the plate. "Sorry, do you want some?

"I ask you to not swear in my home," Thaddeus said. "But please, enjoy the meal. I am not particularly hungry." He prodded the fireplace with a poker, watching the flames grow.

Victor sat on the leather sofa in silence. By the coffee table, he saw a picture frame lying face down. He lifted it, seeing a pictogram of two lovers, hand in hand. Victor almost recognized the handsome man as a younger Thaddeus, long before his augments.

He dared not ask about that.

Meanwhile, Thaddeus put a kettle on the fire, removing his respirator for the first time. Enjoying a cup by himself—Victor had never been fond of tea—the inquisitor was sure to cover his face with a handkerchief, but Victor caught a glimpse of lipless deformity. He could hear Thaddeus wheezing as he sipped.

"So," Thaddeus said, reconnecting the tubes to his lungs. "This is an odd turn of events."

Victor bit into a chocolate truffle, but he didn't reply.

"We haven't had a chance to truly talk." Thaddeus lay his iron hands on his knees, as if looking for a topic of mutual interest. "Are you a student? Where you come from?"

"Part-time," Victor replied.

"That is good to hear," Thaddeus said. "When I was your age, I was taught in the monasteries, where I studied chivalric poetry and calligraphy while my peers preferred swordsmanship. Times were simpler then, as I had—different physical capabilities." He tapped a finger on the table. "School days are an important part of a young man's life."

Victor cracked a coy smile. "I get that a lot."

"Do not sacrifice friendships for the sake of studies," Thaddeus added. "It is important to enjoy life, especially while you're still young—and free."

The mood grew dour. Victor looked away.

Thaddeus sighed. "My apologies. I am not one for small talk. And I am sure you have better things to do than listen to an old fool's lectures."

"I don't mind," Victor lied.

"I understand if you hate me," Thaddeus said. "To you,

Holy Gothica must be a terrifying place. But for now, we will endure each other's company. I must find the culprit. You must find your friends. Our fates are intertwined. Let us take advantage of it."

"I don't hate you." Victor meant that much.

"I am glad." If Thaddeus could smile, Victor knew he would have. "Time will tell where this adventure takes us. But for now, consider yourself my acolyte. It will be easier to explain to the Stormtrooper Corps, as opposed to rambling about 'messianic business.'"

Victor gave a nervous laugh.

"Now," Thaddeus said. "Tomorrow I will begin the preparations for our search. I must visit the Departmento Forensis to study our gathered evidence, especially those of leads and suspects, and obtain a warrant to Yoshiwara District."

"How long will all that take?"

"A week at minimum," Thaddeus said matter-of-factly. "Quite possibly two."

"A *week*?" Victor blurted. "What the hell? They could be dead by then!"

Thaddeus was shocked. Victor turned away, realizing his faux pas.

"S-sorry," he said. "It's just— A lot can happen in that time."

"I know," Thaddeus admitted, "However, I must obey the protocol of Empress and Ecclesiarchy, lest I violate that trust. I must work within the law."

"I thought *you were* the law."

"I do not write the Imperial Creed. I only enforce it," Thaddeus said. "I do not expect you to understand, Victor. Not when you are so unfamiliar with this nation of mine." He stood up. "However, I must ask something of you."

I knew this was coming.

"Do not leave this apartment without me." Thaddeus's voice was stern. "I know what you are thinking. Do *not*. Holy Gothica is filled with danger, much of which you have not yet seen. I know you are concerned for your friends' safety; however, to venture alone would be suicide."

Victor glanced at the grandfather clock. "It's getting really late."

"So it is." Thaddeus's joints creaked like a tin can. "The guest room is the first door on the right." He walked down the hall towards the stairs to the cellar, and stared at Victor for a moment, a moist glimmer in his eyes. "Sleep well."

"You too, Thaddeus."

#

Victor entered the guest room, locking the door behind him. His disturbance masked only by exhaustion, he collapsed on a bed of cotton sheets and feather pillows. Victor made sure to turn away from the window. His head still pounded from that encounter as he dug through his pockets, pulling out his smartphone, an older black model.

No service. What a surprise.

The battery was at two percent as he flipped through his photos — memories of the Waking World. They were mostly shots Charles had taken during their many pub crawls. His heart grew heavy as he looked over a few of their messages.

dude i forgot! happy 21st! drinks at g street? first round on me XD

Victor sighed. He didn't know what depressed him more — Charles's heinous grammar or his own regrets. Regardless, his fingers slid over the touchscreen, reading,

Not tonight, I have school tomorrow.

tomorrows Saturday:

So it is. I'll be there in fifteen minutes.

groovy

There were many more like that. Nameless numbers, potential friendships he'd pushed away, and failed attempts at flirting, all leading to the lonely doldrums of mediocrity. To think, a few hours ago Victor had been a college student on his way home from the bars. Now he was trapped in a nightmare of cathedrals and serial killers. A world of disturbing familiarity.

Then, the screen went black.

Victor put his toy rabbit on the night table. He stared into its marble eye at his own reflection. Mind wandering, he turned to an aquarium built into the wall that was filled with silver sardines, swimming in a spiral. Victor smiled, remembering his own fish tank and the visits with Mother to the bay when he was growing up. Back in the Waking World. It was hardly an hour's drive from town, during a time when his autism shone like a beacon of eccentricity. He'd only learned to work around that, using a handful of niche skills to his advantage.

Touching the little creatures in the pools. Watching towering kelp sway behind glass. Smiling. Always going to gray beaches afterwards, and maybe getting a bowl of clam chowder at the wharf, simmered with an innocence that had died long ago. Its memory was a rotting corpse at the back of his mind. He wished to relive those joys, but whenever he returned to those shores, he saw only a gravestone of youth, and felt the grief of maturity.

What am I doing with my life?

Victor's eyelids grew heavy, fading into deepest slumber before he knew it. Then he saw that mental sanctuary: baroque, blue, and all too familiar.

The Opera House?

He was lying on his side and hoisted himself up, engulfed

by numbing lucidity. Hanging along the walls were a series of elegant masks, all silver and gold. Victor saw the curtains scroll up, blinded by light again. He did not look away, not this time. He squinted at a silver screen until the theater dimmed, and Victor made out a shadow upon the stage—a wheelchair of chrome, a lone figure bound to its cushions.

Victor took a step back, unsettled by the caretaker.

He was a bizarre man of ambiguous age—not quite human. His diminutive stature was childlike, and yet a wrinkled face gave him a sagely quality. With a face of porcelain and a long, pointed nose, his grin was far too wide. Dressed in a velvet suit and a violet tie, his eyes were unblinking, giving away his nature as the proprietor of the cornerstone of cosmos.

"Do not be alarmed." The Impresario's lips moved but his teeth did not. "Your body is fast asleep in Holy Gothica, and your mind is safe here. Long has the Opera House stood as a symbol of your sanity. Such a pity, its current state. Do you remember it now?"

"Yes." Victor cradled his head. "I remember when I was happier."

"Can you tell me when that was?"

"What are you, my therapist?" Victor looked away. "If you're me, you should know."

"If I am you, then you should have no problem telling me," the Impresario retorted.

"I know you're behind everything," Victor snapped. "You summoned me here, and branded me with this eldritch power. Now it's time you told me what's going on."

"Oftentimes, evil makes the first move. Remember your nightmare? That was not my doing, I promise you. And if you remember, that very evil dragged you here, as I awakened your nascent power." The Impresario shuffled a deck of the Imperial

Tarot. He spread a line of cards face down on the podium, and clasped his wrists. "Never once did I take my gaze off you while guiding you through the Music of the Spheres. Would you like to know why?"

"I need to know why."

"You never grew up," the Impresario sighed. "Though you believe you have. And deep down, you know I speak the truth. The ensuing grief, that is the root of all evil within and without. And you are in denial of it. Why else would your own world twist images and respites from youth until they cry out in pain? I awakened you for a reason."

"Survival?" Victor hissed. "I'm working on it."

"Our opponent is the very darkness I speak of—a darkness that will murder you in this fantasy all too real. I am simply a mirror of your will to order. Nothing more and nothing less." He drew a card, face up, revealing the Moon Arcana. That card shimmered with holy light as the image of Dante, the rabbit-eared knight, was projected upon the theater's screen. "But you already knew that. As for your power, it is only just awakening."

Victor stared at his other self. "What do you mean? And what is a geist? I know it's tied to me and the Music of the Spheres. But how does that translate to—you know, superpowers?"

"Geists are born from stories that men have told since the dawn of civilization, taking on archetypal forms. Though the time of mythology is fleeting, so rises an era of literature and cinema. Who is to say their current forms are not evolutions of such high concepts?"

"Like the Divine Comedy?" Victor smiled. "Hang on, does that even exist here?"

"Why should the icons of your passions and livelihood not ripple into your innermost world?" The Impresario twiddled his thumbs. "They are all gods in a pantheon of inspiration, having incarnations in this world's media. You need only know where to look."

"And the cards," Victor asked. "They're just a totem for all this?"

The Impresario laid a hand over the deck. "You are learning quickly. As one chosen by this power, you have access to what many only dream of. The Music of the Spheres flows through you, and thus, the geist is the instrument through which you express it." With that, Dante's image faded, and the silver screen dimmed altogether. "Indeed, this is a dream so deep it has a merit of its own. You do well to remember that."

Victor looked away. "I will. But—"

"Where are your friends? Why are they here? Dragged with you into this world?"

"Yes. What did they do?"

"Nothing." The Impresario shrugged. "I had no role in your descent, and that is the truth. Your friends were in the wrong place at the wrong time. However, a trio of wayward souls in a dying world? That may be enough to unravel the fabric of fate." He nodded. "But tell me, do you believe that you are chosen? That you are the Far Messiah?"

"Well, I haven't made a 'choice' for myself since I arrived. And the moment I'm able to, I'll leave." Victor said that without a second thought. "Even after I find my friends, then what?"

"You would condemn this place to chaos and ruin? For the comforts of mediocrity?"

"I—" Victor mulled over his next words carefully, but something welled inside him that he didn't want to change. He wanted happiness and home. "Yes, I would. Know why? I'm not what you think I am. Gods, kings, heroes—fuck that. I'm going to die here unless I find a way out."

The Impresario's smile faded. "The choice is yours, and

yours alone. And you will accept the consequences when the time comes. For not even gods can outrun the truth."

With that, the Opera House faded. Victor tried to call out, to have the last word, but he was shut out by the Wall of Sleep. When his eyes rolled open, the sun had not yet risen. Regardless, Victor made his choice, stomach sinking with the weight of uncertainty.

Am I a bad person?

That was a question only he could answer. Although he tossed and turned, Victor's conscience forced him awake. Against his better judgment, he rolled out of bed holding the toy rabbit by a stitched arm, like a child in the dark. His footsteps were silent over the beige carpet as he opened the door and crept down the hallway.

What do I do now?

Victor glanced into a few rooms—some locked, others vacant—but Thaddeus was nowhere to be found. And then he came to a bitter realization.

Time is running out. Charles. Beatrice. They're going to die, and Thaddeus can't do anything about it. Not while he's trapped in red tape. And I can't just stay here. I can't do nothing. But—could I escape? If I really wanted to, could I find them? On my own?

The color drained from Victor's face. He knew what to do.

Heart pounding, he glanced at the front door. No. That would be too obvious. Victor had to be clever. His eyes fell upon the staircase, where Thaddeus had made his descent for reasons unknown. The inquisitor was either still there, or doing business in the City Above.

Victor took a deep breath and gathered his wits.

Clenching the wooden railing, he descended those stairs as the warmth and comfort of the apartment vanished. At the concrete bottom Victor saw an iron door, barely ajar, leading into a basement of utter blackness. Despite an overwhelming sense of dread he kept moving, feeling his way along the walls. The door slammed and locked itself behind him. A series of eerie lights flashed on, revealing the sinister headquarters Victor had first envisioned.

Nowhere to go but forward.

CHAPTER TEN

The laboratory reeked of bleach and smoke, a haze so thick Victor could have cut it with a knife. Dim lights flickered overhead, distorted by rotating fans, and the tiles were stained with unknown chemicals. Its bizarre machines were largely unseen, and yet, against the grayness, Victor saw the shadows of tall monitors and racks of hacksaws and twisted instruments.

I have to be careful. God knows what Thaddeus keeps locked up here.

Listening to the purring engines, Victor knew he was being watched, but dared not look back. He imagined the inquisitor turning the corner, staring him dead in the face. Still, Victor thought it odd how Thaddeus evoked such respect yet such terror. Maybe it was Stockholm Syndrome—or maybe it was the start of a deeply dysfunctional friendship.

What the hell was that?!

Something clanged past Victor—something cumbersome and mechanical. He spun around, eyes widening upon an operating table, where the chirurgeons leered. Such labori were draped in clerical cowls, as hunchbacks of flesh and fused iron. Victor made out tubes jutting from their hidden faces. They clicked in a binary tongue, ignoring the intruder, polishing a set of iron limbs with sponges and whirligig digits.

Wait — are those Thaddeus's prosthetics?

Distracted by sinew and steel, Victor's knee slammed into a desk. Stifling a painful groan, he noticed a board of photos and labels. It was devoted to the murders and suspicious persons near, "Yoshiwara District." He recognized a few names and key terms — Lady Fukuhara, telephone poles, surgical precision — and, of course, the Dollmaker.

A mind map, by the look of it.

There was a recurring image in these sepia pictures — dolls. Victor understood why, but it was still unsettling. From the photos of masked victims to old toys that looked disturbingly similar, it was apparent that Thaddeus was desperate to find any correlation.

Upon closer inspection, Victor saw another set of photos, cast over a wrinkled file, titled, "OUTSIDERS." No doubt these were taken from the Vox Networks. Flipping through them, his eyes widened, recognizing a middle-aged man with flowing silver hair.

Charles? So, he made it after all.

Victor smiled. He had never disbelieved Thaddeus, but seeing this evidence brought him one step closer to the reunion. The photos were all "classified," the most recent taken two weeks ago. Nothing relating to Beatrice could be found, and yet hope kindled in Victor's soul.

The whirl of a drill jolted him, and Victor felt the chirurgeons' gaze.

All right. Don't get ahead of yourself. You need to get out of here first.

Turning his head, he saw a dusky plaque by the desk holding a shillelagh of old. Its shaft was engraved with lyrics and notes, handle marked with a bass clef—a relic of musical magi.

Yeah, I definitely need some kind of weapon.

Gripping the shaft, he twisted the top, revealing a sword hidden in the wood, shimmering against the lights. And yet, conflicting thoughts flooded Victor's mind.

This isn't right, stealing from Thaddeus. But I guess I'll have to make some "moral adjustments" if I want to survive down here.

A floodlight sparked on, bathing the laboratory in fluorescent light. It shined upon a cylindrical tank, filled with cloudy water—an incubator of piston and pump. Its bottom was covered by a tangled mass of tubes, while the placard above read,

RENOVATIO TANK

Squinting, Victor saw a silhouette behind the glass—a muscular amputee, cables and wires jutting from iron sockets, suspending the figure in the frothing gloom. His head was bowed, and his face covered by a rebreather. Victor recognized the disfigured man at once.

Thaddeus? Is that how you sleep?

There the inquisitor floated, stripped of his armor and arms—as a newborn on life support. Victor shuddered at the hibernating officer, planting the blackthorn cane against the tiles until he saw a passage leading ever deeper into the complex. The labori were still staring at him, unblinking and unmoving. Then Victor mustered the last of his courage and crept as quietly as he could, driven by the promise of freedom.

#

The tiles were a grayscale mosaic of shattered clockworks. All was wreathed in dust, for not even the labori bothered to clean these corridors. As the lights faded, Victor felt a tingle at the back of his skull—a static of unknown origin, broadcasting a concerto on the stagnant air.

Wait, I recognize these instruments –

Victor tapped to the tempo as a choir echoed in his mind's ear. They were voices independent of his own, yet nonetheless bound to a shared nostalgia. Cobalt flames lit along the walls, cased in glass ossuaries, dancing above bones. He recalled the Vaults of Prayer, where the dreams of the masses were archived.

Perhaps this was no different.

Victor shut his eyes, walking down the long way, listening to the music all the while. A guitar carried the first canto, strumming the sweet leitmotif of his earliest memory. It was the song his father had used to serenade his wife-to-be, passed on from young love to their child.

And so, the choir said, as if narrating a time before Victor's birth,

In the beginning, we knew nothing, save the reign of chaos,
We drifted in ignorance and doubt, in the blackness of infinity,
We suffered a hollow existence, in anarchy and lightlessness,
And we knew neither good nor evil, in the silence of apathy.

Then a second guitar joined in, carrying an evolution of the lullaby. It was Victor's first composition, conceived when he was six. He remembered the look of awe on his father's face when he played it for the first time, and Victor had never stopped composing since. This rendition built and built, yet was always unfinished.

And yet, in the heat of our despair, the great egg was incubated,
By our turmoil, it hatched with the brilliance of hope,
Our cries were quelled by moon and star, by the first song,
And from that sacred order, Our Child found a cradle of cosmos.

Violins and violas joined the undercurrents, signing and sighing, reminiscent of Tchaikovsky. Victor gave a bittersweet chuckle. When he was ten, Mother had taken him to see *The*

109

Nutcracker. They'd had front row seats, close enough to see the lead's "nuts" bulging in those pastel tights. They did not hold back laughter, but that fateful night had changed the way Victor perceived and wrote his music, and obsession only grew from there.

Then, the twin guitars carried a third canto to happier heights.

His flaming boleros created the red earth, giving us home,
His serenades of starlight divided night and day, giving us law,
His minuets breathed feeling into our souls, giving us life,
And he ended every movement with just respite.

Insular as he was, many people had inspired Victor's growing work—strangers and friends, like it or not. It was everywhere he looked: in musty tomes at the library, and long visits to the art gallery. The ballad continued, now with woodwinds and brass, dueling yet diving together, forming a symphony of diversity as the concerto reached a peak in its harmony.

Our Child dreamed of divine servitors, the geists,
Beings of holy light, to lead the people in the way of peace,
They spread His gospel through song and hymn – oaths to order,
And then, he set out, to bring Heaven unto Earth, and joy unto
all.

With a sudden snare the music turned somber—a sad reprise of that main theme. It was when imagination lay broken by the trials of adolescence. Victor had always had a keen, if linear, sense of time. He knew, come what may, these golden days would end, as childhood would be corroded from his soul. Slowly, Victor's heart turned bitter as he tried to grow up.

His work had long suffered for it, and it would never fully recover.

But then, Our Child's strength ran out, for he too aged,

He collapsed before the gates, and all wept for His passing,
Wonder left the world, as the gardens of hope turned gray,
He became one with His music, memory fleeting yet eternal.

Friendless and insufferable, Victor had learned to mask his loneliness through a perversion of self-care: narcissism. He didn't need people. What good were they? All they brought him was suffering. He was better off with his music. Alone. After all, he *was* destined for greatness.

That was what Victor had once told himself.

He knew better now. Just as the artist needs a muse, so does the self need others. The intermezzo continued, until it slowly rose into a crescendo of Victor's current compositions.

A tear trickled down his face, and he carried on.

And so, Our Child is not lost, echoing through this ballad,
He drifts in ignorance and doubt beyond, among far stone towers,
He suffers an age of melancholy and maturity, but not with hope,
And we too pray, that one day, He will usher His Kingdom of
Ends.

So, it ended. Victor opened his reddening eyes, giving a sigh. The long hall was behind him, and yet he still felt naked in the dark. Uncertainty weighed on him. In the end, what could he really do? Victor took a deep breath. It was like standing before a great cliff. Not only did he fear falling off, but of plummeting of his own accord, possessed by suicide.

I have a choice – I always did.

Victor felt hope kindling in the abyss consuming him. All those pulp novels and epics, the ones where everything looked grim. This was no different. This was Victor's story, and it was only just beginning. Although he did not realize it then, the choice was already made.

I'm going to find my friends. After that, we'll see what happens.

When his mind cleared, Victor saw a nave at the labyrinth's

end. Gaudy and garish, it was beyond compare, more like a concert hall than any cathedral. The statues lining its walls were angelic figures, each holding an instrument — an orchestra of saints. Behind the altar was a doorway of brass and ivory, looming as a threshold of salvation, while further above were six stained glass windows, all opulent and imperial. Victor squinted at the rays of dawn light beyond them, wondering what this strange world's sun was like.

"So, you are trying to escape upon first light." Victor's heart leapt up his chest as Thaddeus stepped from the shadows, clad in his trench coat and military uniform, armed with his iron prosthetics. "I am disappointed," the inquisitor said, "but not surprised."

#

The silence seemed to last forever. Thaddeus stood between Victor and the way out, tall and unwavering. And yet, Victor felt a scarlet wave of guilt. He was caught. No more tricks. No more lies. No going back. He would own up to this decision.

"Thaddeus—" Victor held back a nervous twitch. "I—"

"I do not blame you," the inquisitor said. "However, you must listen to reason. There shall come a time when we will save your friends, but it is not now." He turned to the doorway. "This path will eventually take you to the deepest catacombs of this City Above. From there, it is a treacherous descent, starting from the Iron Sky back to the serfdoms."

"I assumed so." Victor tried to rise past his fear. "But that changes nothing."

"I see." Thaddeus's eyes fell upon Victor's sword cane. "Have you ever wielded one?"

"I took a class." Even then, Victor knew Gothic swordplay and modern fencing were very different things. His fingers wrapped around the toy rabbit. "And I have that power. I'll be *fine.*"

"Provident though you may be, your geist cannot best every foe. It is bound to the Music of the Spheres alone. Outside the intervention of daemonic surges, you are utterly mortal."

Victor's fear churned in a cesspool of frustration. "I have to do this."

"The conviction of a fool," Thaddeus said. "If you cross this threshold and return to the slums, you will be killed. If you truly wish to see your friends again, you will wait."

"And what should I do in the meantime?" Anger boiled in Victor's chest. "Just loiter in the high castle? Until we get a lead or another body shows up?"

"Yes," Thaddeus said bluntly.

Victor was shaking. "Get out of the way, Thaddeus. *Now.*"

"Ungrateful brat," Thaddeus muttered, laying a hand on a belt pouch, withdrawing those runic knuckles. "You do not understand. I meant it when I said I would protect you. I am a man of my word." He rubbed his metal fingers against the bones. "However, I know your pain, and so—" He tossed them in the air, and they clattered onto his palm. "I—"

"What do they say this time?" Victor asked. "What does it come down to?"

"They say," Thaddeus hesitated, lowering his head, "that I must put you to the test." With that, he swung his sword and electro-staff wide and akimbo, sparking as tesla coils of arcane power. The hairs on Victor's neck stood on edge. He took a step back as Thaddeus's mechanical breaths filled the air. "Prove to me your potential," Thaddeus said. "Only then will you pass."

Victor shuddered. There was no reasoning with the inquisitor. He was in the way, and violence was the only language these fascists understood. And yet, it pained Victor to look at his jailor this way. In another place and time, could things have turned out differently? Perhaps so. But in the here and now, Thaddeus was yet another obstacle to be overcome.

Charles — Beatrice. I'm coming.

Victor rushed with a furious cry, twisting the cane's hilt, unsheathing his sword, only to be met with a blinding flash of electricity. He was sent flying in the air by crackling force, wracked by spasms of agony. He screamed, skidding on his back, as Thaddeus stood his ground.

"D—dammit," Victor wheezed, joints contracting as he stood. "How in the hell—?"

Thaddeus remained silent, beckoning with an iron hand.

When Victor regained the courage he lunged once more. With a shaky parry the next electro-bolt bounced off his blade. Victor smiled. He remembered the fencing courses he'd taken with Charles just last year. The two were "Flynning" it, and—

J-jesus fuck!

Victor's knees buckled with a numbing buzz, mind fried by white pain. Thaddeus loomed over him. Was this really worth it? Was there another option? Victor thought it over, but an image of Charles impaled on a telephone pole flashed in his mind. He gritted his teeth until he thought they might break. He rose, again, and the duel went on.

Victor swayed to and fro, vision blurred by exhaustion and adrenaline. Thaddeus paced about until their swords met again and locked. Pressing down, the inquisitor's iron strength made Victor quake, holding that blade with both hands.

"Impressive," Thaddeus admitted. "But against the enemy, you can afford no quarter." He pushed, almost buckling Victor with weight alone. "You are still a novice."

Their eyes locked until Victor saw a glimmer of fettered conflict in his opponent. With a burst of finesse, he unlocked their blades and knocked Thaddeus's sword out of his hand. It landed with a clatter on the floor. Victor gave a cock-eyed grin.

"Take your own damn advice," he said. "I'm not here for a lecture on chivalry."

Wow, I actually pulled that off —

With a crack and a crunch, Victor was on his back again. This time his nose throbbed and gushed, as if hit by a ton of metal. Thaddeus's steel knuckle was splashed with blood.

"N-not fair," Victor sputtered.

"The slums and gangers are not fair," Thaddeus said. "The Dollmaker and the daemons are not fair. *Life* is not fair. If you expect mercy from the enemy, then you are a fool." Another blast of electricity came hurtling Victor's way, but he rolled aside and snatched his sword, jerking it up with a stagger. "Are we done yet?" Thaddeus growled.

Victor spat and wiped the blood off his battered nose. Now he was angry. He paced about, light on his quivering feet, as Thaddeus gave a steam bound sigh.

"You're holding back." Victor blocked another series of blows. "I can tell."

"Should I not, you would be dead where you stand." Thaddeus raised his voice. "Why will you not listen? Why muster such strength for this futile endeavor?"

"It's what *friends* do."

"Listen." Thaddeus words turned a tad softer. "I know this is not ideal, Victor. But you cannot charge blindly into the unknown. This is for your own good — "

"Bullshit!" Victor snapped, swinging that sword over his head.

Thaddeus blocked that with ease, slamming a jackboot against Victor's chest, knocking the wind clean out of him. He lowered his head. "Was that meant to be fatal?"

Victor couldn't speak, barely able to stand. Leaning on his

sword, coated in his own blood, he glowered at his captor. And yet, Victor trudged through the tremors and pain.

I won't let them go that easily.

"For Heaven's sake, Victor," Thaddeus barked. "Why? Why do you insist on doing this?" He stepped forward. "What the devil are you proving this way?"

They're all I have left.

Another electro-bolt blasted past Victor's head, singeing the ends of his hair. He cracked a weak smile as Thaddeus's words began to slur, bouncing off his ringing ears.

"Stop it," Thaddeus cried, all but pleading. "I know you want to see your friends. More than anything. To know whether they are safe. But you cannot do this alone." Droplets trickled down Thaddeus's face, but whether tears or sweat, Victor could not tell. "Please, give me more time."

Volley after volley, Thaddeus shot, but Victor kept walking.

That's not going to happen.

"Dammit." The inquisitor looked away. "Why must you make this so difficult? If you go out there alone, you *will* die. Can you not understand, or do you simply not care?"

I don't know anymore.

Victor was inches from Thaddeus's face, staring him dead in the eye, though he could barely see, until the inquisitor lowered to his ward's level.

"I know." Thaddeus gave a sad chuckle. "I know now. You have certainly proven one thing. Unskilled as you are, you cannot be easily swayed. Even by force. For whether stupidity or sheer determination, it is…." He paused. "Respectable. Truly respectable."

The world swirled around Victor, and he collapsed to his knees. The inquisitor had bested him, and yet, Victor knew a point had been made. The last he remembered, Thaddeus hoisted his limp arm over an iron shoulder, dragging him away. Then all went black.

CHAPTER ELEVEN

When Victor awoke, he was submerged in cloudy water, a gentle reverb filling his ears. He gasped—an oxygen mask covered his face. Thaddeus stood outside the tank, iron arms crossed. Victor's heart pounded. This was the laboratory. Was he being experimented on for his defiance? Injected with mutagens? Vivisected? Regardless, a sharp monitor beeped in tune with his heart, and the inquisitor walked to a far control panel.

"Condition stabilized," a staticky voice said. "Restoration at one-hundred percent."

Wait — did he heal me?

The beeping slowed, and Victor felt no pain. When the vacuum hatch opened he floated upward, lifted out of the water by those spidery chirurgeons. He was dripping wet, yet rejuvenated. As Victor staggered down those mesh steps, Thaddeus tossed him a warm towel.

"H-how long was I out?" Victor managed, wiping his face.

"I took care not to injure you severely," Thaddeus replied. "The Renovatio Tank healed your wounds over the course of four hours. Your broken cartilage took the longest to reconstruct.

118

The cosmetic damage is minimal, save for a bit of scarring."

Victor touched his nose. It was as if nothing happened — at least, physically.

"You fought gallantly," Thaddeus said. "I did not expect such perseverance. I all but crippled you, and yet you kept rising, again and again."

"Like I said, it's what friends do."

"Your definition of friendship is most intriguing." Thaddeus's eyes glistened with perplexity. "Regardless, what you feel is love. A will to do good. To protect those in need." He bowed his head. "You would make an excellent inquisitor."

Victor didn't know how to respond.

"If you care for them that much," Thaddeus said. "I have no right to stand in your way."

"Wait." Victor's eyes widened. "Are you — ?"

"Letting you go?" Thaddeus scoffed. "Don't be absurd. Valor alone does not make one a soldier of order. However, I will not let the Ecclesiarchy tether us to pointless protocol."

"What about the Empress?" Victor asked. "She sounded pretty serious."

"I will do what I can," Thaddeus replied. "But first, we must gather information regarding your friends' whereabouts. This much my superiors will understand. For we are on a missing persons case, unrelated to the serial murders. At least, thus far."

A labori handed Victor his clothes, folded and pressed.

"By the way, what *is* this place?" he asked, "Some kind of training ground?"

"Indeed. This laboratory has not seen use in quite some time, ever since its covert programs were cancelled by the Ecclesiarchy. Among other things."

When Victor put on his trench coat, propping the collar, he glanced into the chirurgeon's eyes — the eyes of a lobotomized heretic. He shuddered. Although an oppressive theocracy, this was a world where religion had more than symbolic merit. The result was hardly "angelic," and he had a feeling Thaddeus knew that all too well.

"You don't really think it's right, do you? What you people do?" Victor remembered the destitution below. "This poverty, this violence, this — fascism."

Thaddeus stared back, eyes glazed with shock. "Those are dangerous words, Victor. Those less understanding would call it heresy. However, I forgive your transgression of faith, for your words are not — untrue. At any rate, do not mistake me for a slave of the state, Victor. You said it yourself once — I *am* the law." He nodded, turning to the door. "Now, clean yourself up. We leave whenever you are ready."

#

Shortly thereafter, they returned to the Apostolic Palace. Thaddeus made preparations in the sanctioned library, while Victor sat in a nearby drawing room. Scribbling melodies on a napkin, he ran his fingers through his hair, trying to distract himself from the dangers ahead.

I can't even write a good prelude here.

Crumpling the paper, Victor tossed it towards the wastebasket. It bounced off the rim, like the others. Mind wracked with worry, he turned to the bay window, gazing across Holy Gothica and the surrounding badlands; and yet, his mind was elsewhere.

Crossing his legs, Victor read the newspaper of gothic design.

PLAGUE RAVAGES SERFDOMS

The leprosy is hardly news. It is a foodborne illness at first glance, but displays "daemonic" qualities. Since the epidemic, several murders have been recorded near Yoshiwara and the Leper Quarter. Moreover, the Inquisition has suffered outages on their Vox Networks when these killings occur. But perhaps most disturbing of all are the sightings of cryptids dubbed, "daemons." Little official data has been released —

"Victor." He heard someone calling. "Victor Roland."

He spun around to see the Empress herself, escorted by a quartet of gilded knights. She walked with pride as the Lady of the Ecclesiarchy.

"Uh," Victor blathered. "Yes? Your grace...majesty...lord?"

"There is no need to bother with titles. Have you seen Ser Thaddeus?"

"He just went to get a few things. He'll be back soon."

"I see." Johanna looked away. "I beg your pardon, but there is something else. I come to apologize for my behavior earlier. You must understand, as the Holy Pontiff and Empress, I must be uncompromising. Otherwise, many will think me young and naive."

"Oh. It's fine."

Johanna smiled and stepped forward. "I am glad. Far Messiah or not, you are still an outsider, something most rare." She gestured to the window and wastelands. "It is all right, you need not hide it—I am ashamed of this state too. But to an outsider, it must be horrific." She shuddered. "To think my forebears tolerated it."

"I'm not going to lie," Victor said, sighing. "It's a nightmare, literally."

"The Dreamer Within Dreams," Johanna replied. "Perhaps there is merit to Ser Thaddeus's claims. But I cannot risk all in the name of esoteric prophecy, Victor." She looked him in the eye. "The lord-regents were good to me, but cared for little else.

Though they left Holy Gothica in ruins, I shall turn this realm into a respectable nation of men." She smiled, wryly. "By the way, are you accompanying Ser Thaddeus? There is no shame in waiting here."

"I am going," Victor replied. "I don't know why, really. But it's the right thing to do." He considered telling Johanna of his friends, but thought better of it. "If I am the Far Messiah, this is a place of my creation, and I'm responsible for it."

Johanna raised an eyebrow. "Pardon. 'If' you are the Far Messiah?"

"How can I really know?" Victor shrugged. "I mean, it makes sense, I guess. But still, it's a lot of responsibility for one person. Besides, what I am supposed to do? Even if I am?"

"With all due honesty, our holy texts were lost long ago. Only stained glass and placards remain, famed in archaic myth, things we must piece together—"

"Ah, my lady." Thaddeus returned with an old tome. "What brings me the honor?"

"Ser Thaddeus." She handed him an envelope. "I have sent a squad to assist you—the 105th, seeing as you've worked with them in the past. I would spare a full company, but this is a delicate operation." The Empress gave parting words. "Take care, Victor, and should you prove your provident nature, we shall certainly talk again."

With that, Johanna departed, leaving them to their business.

"That went better than I expected," Victor said.

"Indeed." Thaddeus nodded. "Something seemed—off, though."

"What do you mean?"

"Something must have happened regarding the case," he said. "Otherwise, she would not have acted so swiftly. We too must act with a sense of urgency, Victor. Two weeks for gathering resources is standard protocol. If the Empress authenticated our mission before then—" He laid a hand to his chin. "This is most curious."

"Anyway, what did you find?" Victor asked.

"An archive of Doctor Murdoch's confiscated journals." He sighed, laying the book on the table. "Quite disturbing to read firsthand how my friend drifted down the river of madness. However, things were set in motion that cannot be undone." He flipped open the book to a particular entry. "And this passage points to a potential involvement in recent events."

Victor leaned over Thaddeus's shoulder and read the excerpt carefully.

The exact nature of vitae is an esoteric thing. Though an undeniably physical substance, it is the culmination of one's very being, and at the same time, a piece of something far greater. Vitae can best be compared to a shard of stained glass. Without the Symphonia Mundi's light behind it, it is a dull, unassuming object. But when such light shines through vitae, permeating its existence with life and sentience, the illustrations of the ego become apparent, in all its flawed splendor.

It is a truly human thing—Anima Firmatis.

However, one must not mistake the intensity of this light for love, compassion, or good. The truth is something far weirder, yet fundamental. Vitae is bent by the strength of will, by the powers of perseverance and discipline. As the filter between the self and the world, vitae knows only what limits we give it, and if we break those limits, the way forward is one we pave ourselves. Imagine, if we could find a way to replicate or extract this power, and use it as a resource.

Regardless, I am filled with hope and fear for the future.

"Vitae." Victor shuddered, remembering those corpses

in the school, drained of blood, impaled and rigid, doll masks stitched to their faces. "That's what the daemons were collecting."

"One thing is most clear, Victor," Thaddeus replied, shutting the book. "The dark harvest is only beginning, and is, at least in part, inspired by Murdoch's heretical sciences. Though to dismiss all his work would be foolish. He is responsible for my prosthetics and quality of life, for I was a prototype soldier of one of his projects." He lifted his iron fist. "These augments were to make me resistant to the throes of the Cacophony."

"Was your project cancelled too?" Victor asked. "Did something happen?"

Thaddeus looked away, as if he didn't know what to say.

"You don't have to tell me, if it's, you know, 'classified.'"

"That's just it." Thaddeus stared out the window. "I cannot remember what happened. It was before Murdoch's excommunication. But the actual program is a haze. I have no recollection of its therapy or training, only that I must take specific elixirs to maintain my mental health." His eyes glistened with warmth, as if trying to be reassuring. "Do not dwell on such things, Victor. I am an agent of the Inquisition, and I chose whatever path I took. I remember very little, but I believe we were to research the leprosy. I assume it was to find a cure. That is all."

"Have you ever tried to look into it?" Victor asked. "Don't you have, like, archival data?"

"All records were expunged," Thaddeus said. "But the circumstances trouble me deeply. Before the project, Murdoch was not the mad heretic the state remembers today. He was unorthodox and outlandish, but never dangerous. However, after the project's end, he was a raving lunatic, if pitiable. Do not tell anyone that. I suspect that I was not supposed to remember such details. Know that I chose to forget whatever happened." He caressed a bolt jutting from the back of his skull. "And perhaps such things are best left forgotten."

Victor said nothing. Was Thaddeus really so blinded by faith? Or was he masking his skepticism out of fear? Regardless, Victor felt he understood the inquisitor a little more.

"Well," he said, "What do we do now?"

"Now?" Thaddeus replied. "Let us be off. There is a dangerous road ahead."

#

Under a rust-green sky and morning rainfall, Victor and Thaddeus returned to the plaza before the Apostolic Palace, where half a dozen stormtroopers and a few labori greeted them. They clutched halberds and bestrode hairless horses, perhaps a mutant breed of Clydesdales, a Kaiser-helmed captain at their head, tugging at the reins as a noblest officer.

"Ser Thaddeus," she called. "This unit is at your disposal. Where is our heading?"

"Captain Hildegarde, there has been a change of plans." Thaddeus gestured to Victor. "I will take my newfound acolyte with us on this mission, as he requires field experience."

Victor stared into the horse's vacant eyes. "Can't I just walk beside you?"

Hildegarde stifled a chuckle. "Your pardon, ser. But places infested by lepers are no place for the faint of heart, let alone the cowardly. He shall die in shame, I warrant."

"He has already fought against such horror," Thaddeus hissed. "Now, get him a mount."

The inquisitor and the stormtroopers nimbly mounted their steeds, while Victor was hoisted by a labori onto a smaller steed, which was jerky and uncooperative. But Victor was at ease for now, passing by where the Circus of Hours was being constructed and planned.

"Where are we going?" Victor called out. "Yoshiwara?"

"Indeed," Thaddeus replied. "Though be warned. It is a lawless place, where thieves and strumpets prosper under the Inquisition's very nose. Stay close and do not stray."

"Hang on," Victor asked. "Why do you think Charles and Beatrice are there?"

"Because it is not under watch by the Vox Networks," Thaddeus said. "And this 'Charles' character sounds like a hedonist. Also, I believe Leng might be in Yoshiwara as well."

"Leng?" Victor scoffed. "What's he doing there?"

"Inquisitors often have certain liberties, some excluding vows of chastity altogether. And Leng is morally flexible. I require him as intelligence during our investigation."

"I see, but I don't know about this." Victor looked away, remembering the encounter in the abandoned schoolyard. "That outburst with Dante was one thing, but this is something else. I'm not sure I can do this, Thaddeus. I mean, keep up with you and the soldiers."

"Do not be a fool, Victor," Thaddeus interrupted. "I have seen what you are capable of. And you must learn that there is no courage without fear." He glanced at his men, the faceless soldiers of the state. "Remember that, and you will find true bravery."

Victor did not reply, avoiding Thaddeus's gaze.

"At any rate," the inquisitor said, lifting a familiar cane, "this belongs to you."

"O-oh!" Victor's heart jolted, remembering his theft. "Y-yeah. Sorry about—"

"What? That you stole a relic from a sacred vault of the Inquisition? It is true, I had every reason to execute you for that. Save my own code of ethics." He chuckled, handing Victor the

126

shillelagh. "For I believe you will need such a weapon far more than I."

Victor tied the cane to his saddle. "Thank you, Thaddeus."

With a nod, the inquisitor returned to the head of the company. As the squad boarded the Great Lifts upon the city perimeter, Victor gave one last look to the heavens.

It was the sky of another world, alien yet familiar, with its black rain and zeppelins circling the bell towers. The moon shone behind those polluted clouds, leering over all. And yet, Victor felt no fear or awe. Not anymore. Only a cold acceptance of the "reality" of his situation. He smiled bitterly, turning back to Thaddeus, who beckoned him to follow.

Victor knew this odyssey was only just beginning.

CHAPTER TWELVE

Holy Gothica was a city of blood, shit, and diesel.

Here, in a numbered alley, a man waited in silence, a camera dangling around his neck. He picked the glass out of his sliced palms as the black rain of the ductworks fell on his face. It was all a haze of smog, but he was too drunk to care. Behind the screens, whispers filled his ears, rising and falling, serenading his sadism.

Such was the Thirteenth Frequency, thinning the line between worlds.

Televisions provided the perfect window into the other side, large enough to shove a person through. A surge of static filled the air. Unseen daemons shrieked on the speakers, and with a sparking blast, *she* appeared, impaled on the telephone pole. Crimson drops trickled onto the gravel. The streetwalker was covered in puncture wounds, fishnets and leather ripped apart by fang and claw. Her eyes rolled behind the doll mask stitched to her face, twitching her last.

He gazed upon the beauty of death.

Then, a church bell sang over the steeples and shingles. The lights buzzed back on. He blinked — the mundane world resumed. The work was much better in chiaroscuro. Streetlights defiled it, ridding the model of all modesty, revealing its flaws.

He raised his camera and snapped a single photo. A waste of flesh and film. Taking a swig from his flask, he staggered back to the avenues. It was only a matter of time before the stormtroopers would arrive. Along brick-and-mortar apartments, the reek of manure flooded the streets as the people carried on—all piercings and dyed hair. He followed the red paper lanterns to Yoshiwara, to its saloons and sex shops.

His hunting ground.

The streetwalkers cooed and he cringed. Blank film, subjects waiting to be shot. Wading against the currents of pedestrians and parasols, he came to a triple-tiered brothel, the Sunset Pagoda, perfume wafting from its windows. The bouncers nodded, opening the door, and he wandered to the back bar, ordering his usual—a straight shot of absinthe.

A high alarm echoed in the distance. The Dollmaker smiled.

#

It had been two weeks since that murder—not that Charles could remember, especially at the bar. With a deep green peacoat lying on another stool, his only companions were a revolver and a bottle of gin, reflection distorted by liquor. In Yoshiwara, it was all one could get for a few coppers during "happy hour," fusing to his throat like hot tar—but it made him almost forget.

Almost....

"Here you go, sweetheart." A serving girl in a corset came to his side. "The 'this n' thats,' and another pint of the porter." Her rosy cheeks glistened. "Anything else?"

"Thanks." Charles ran a hand through his silver hair. "But—I don't remember ordering a beer." His stomach dropped. "How's my tab holding up?"

"It's on the bartender. You're a regular. Anything else I can get you?"

"I haven't been here *that* long." Charles looked away at his munchies. A small platter of goat cheese, dried fruits, and bread—little comforts, reminding him of home. "Have I?"

"A month straight." Her brow furrowed. "Are you feeling okay?"

"I'm alright-a." Charles passed her a few gear-shaped coins. "Again, thanks."

When the barmaid left him, Charles was alone with his thoughts. In his pocket, he rubbed his fingers against a pair of tie-dye dice, or "2d6," as tabletop gamers called it.

It was a memento of the mundane life—the life he'd left behind.

Now Charles was dressed in a burgundy suit, unwashed hair drooped over his face, glasses snowy with dandruff. At times Charles heard voices in his skull, reminiscent of those bad trips from way back when, coming from the talisman—a conduit for a greater power.

Do you remember, Charles? Do you remember as it used to be?

He gritted his teeth. "Not in the mood for this."

You cannot hide forever. But I cannot force awakening and enlightenment upon you. The strength required to face oneself cannot be mimicked.

He tucked the dice behind a handkerchief, as if trying to muffle them. Jazz on the radio filled his ears, as cigarette smoke loomed over the saloon like a fog of tobacco. Not to mention, the jargon of barflies was never conducive to problem drinking,

"Did ya hear? The Dollmaker struck again."

"Say what? A hooker, I warrant."

"A bunch of 'em, dumped in Jericho's old schoolyard."

"Yeah, them girls here in Yoshiwara have been...."

Another murder. Charles shuddered. His Walkman was running out of juice, but Jimi Hendrix tuned it all out. Considering his day job as a curator, it was a wonder he could pay rent, let alone get new batteries. Alkaline was expensive here too.

One month. It may as well be one year.

He remembered the world he'd left behind, Earth, and how much he'd taken for granted. Just a drifting comedian, going from one job to the next, never looking back. Bartender, physical therapist—hell, he was even an acupuncturist for a month.

At least he had been free.

The world was his oyster, roaming from country to country. What happened to that spark of life? That mojo? What was the Yoko Ono that disbanded his Beatles?

I grew up.

Now the world was a blur of browns, grays, and red lights—a dystopia of diesel and ducts. Working nine to five was as fun as it sounded. Charles had no idea how he had descended this far, let alone how he got here. Shackled to a desk, typing away at an analog computer, a surveillance camera in his face, dealing with historical revisions and five-minute lunches, it was like *Nineteen-Eighty-Four*. Sticking it to the man was all rhetoric. Like he'd told Victor, "Sooner or later, you have to do shit." Even if it was shit he'd rather not do.

Fuck, what I wouldn't give for a puff of real weed. Stuff here's not the same.

Taking a break and rolling a spliff, he smirked at how Victor would have reacted. He was a good kid, a little stiff and straight-edged, but cool. Friends came and went, but it seemed like Victor would stick around. Probably because they both had nowhere else to go.

Tears…?

131

He thought those had dried up long ago, but here they trickled. Not many, but enough to make him realize just how much he missed that dumbass.

"You doing okay there, Charles?" asked a voice, familiar and feminine. "You've been like this since we got dumped here."

Charles barely looked up, seeing Beatrice just past the swinging doors. The long month had not been kind to her either, but she did not stay confined to Holy Gothica.

With short raven hair and ivory skin, she was dressed like a road warrior, constantly off on salvaging trips across the Gotland Wastes, clad in stitches and scraps, armed with unpolished gauntlets and thigh-high combat boots. Something out of a post-apocalyptic thriller. Funny that someone half Charles's age could hold her own better than he ever could.

"Hey." She snapped her fingers in his face. "You okay?"

"Groovy."

"Bullshit." Beatrice rolled her eyes, face almost as grim as his. "You look like a zombie. Been getting worse every day. Wanna talk about it?" She sat down. "I'm all ears."

Charles turned to a red and gold poster on the wall.

IGNITE A BRIGHTER FUTURE
JOIN THE POWDER KEGS

He scoffed. Bombing missions and guerilla warfare? Yeah, right. The only things bright about that were Molotov cocktails. And, by some misguided sense of self-righteousness, Beatrice was one of their sell swords.

"Hey." She leaned in closer, staring into his glazed eyes. "Charles."

The aging hipster rolled his eyes, planting his brow in his hands. He felt the world spin and swirl like a drunken orbit, and he shuddered to think of what tomorrow held.

"Why?" he sighed. "What's there to talk about? You know the deal—we fell from the sky, and the state doesn't like that. Victor probably died in the wreck. Goddammit." He rubbed his brow. "This is pathetic. I'm hiding in the man's red tape, and you're a merc for the terrorists. If it weren't for the fake I.D., I'd probably be crucified by now."

"Yeah, we both would." She pulled out a clove. "The Powder Kegs aren't half bad though. If this goes well, we might even be able to get out of here. Remember—"

"You're up," the bartender grunted. "Hey, Charlie-boy."

"Yeah, I heard you." Charles stood up, pushing in his stool. "Anyway, gotta go."

"Comedy again?" Beatrice gave a coy smile. "After last week—"

"Fuck that." Charles shuddered, fiddling with an empty box of smokes. "I've moved on. Less dick jokes. More class." With that he dropped the box, only to lift his palm at the perfect speed, the pack sticking to his fingers. "Stage magic's in now."

"Magic?" Beatrice's smile faded. "Really, dude?"

"Please, everyone loves a little heresy-lite." He finished the drink in a sticky gulp. "Yeah, gotta go cast some spells and wet some panties."

Charles gave a bitter smile, like a soldier going over the top. He turned his back, walking onstage with as much dignity as he could muster. And when he got there, blinded by harsh light, he was met with piercing glares and judging silence.

"Alright-a." Charles cleared his throat, jaded yet dignified. "I got three minutes, so I'll make it quick. One of you has to come up here." He scanned the crowd, drawing a deck of tarot cards. No one stood up. "That's okay. I have a backup plan."

Always do.

Charles put away the deck and donned his Walkman. The

bums looked at him like he was a freak. He drowned their murmurs with a fast forward to The Lemon Pipers — the music of *his* spheres. Clutching the dice behind his back as a new-wave totem, Charles held up a spoon, twirling it in his fingers, moving it faster and faster.

He heard a murmur of delight, distorted by rewiring synapses, as the spoon hung suspended in the air. It was a different kind of high. His eyes were clenched shut, and the music flickered like psychedelic stars beyond his eyelids. Charles could feel the spoon in his mind, digging into his pupils. He misfired his neurons, and the image in his mind shattered into a thousand pieces, as did the utensil, pieces raining to the floor, met with applause.

The bartender tapped at his pocket watch, giving a nod of approval.

"Well guys, it looks like my time is up. Thanks for watching and putting up with me." Charles smiled as reality returned. "See you all next week." He leapt off the stage, walking back to the bar and Beatrice. "Haven't felt like that since Burning Man."

"That's some weird shit." She smiled, impressed. "How'd you do it?"

"Honestly?" Charles clutched his bottle again. "I've no idea."

Back to his drinks, Charles was distracted. Between praise and booze, it wasn't long before the world was a spinning stupor again. With one earphone on, "Purple Haze" blared on full blast. Leaning on the counter, eyes rolling to the back of his head, Beatrice's words bounced off his eardrums, save for one phrase.

"But I got news."

"Yeah. I heard about the dead hooker."

"*Good* news."

"Here? In the, 'Holy Victorian Reich?'" Charles gave a weak smile, lowering the volume. The song was almost over anyway. "What's up?"

"Another sighting." Beatrice puffed a bit from her second clove, chuckling. "Turns out the Inquisition was dispatched to hunt down someone *else* who fell from the Iron Sky." She slipped him a newspaper article with a blurred photo. "Look familiar? Black hair, tall, skinny, trench coat? Reminds me of him, last seen at Serfdom One"

Charles's heart froze. It was Victor—no mistaking it. His mind went blank—shocked, plain and simple, and yet his spirit was flooded with courage. Serfdom One was the next district over, just past the Grinning Gates. He was shaking, as the archaic voice returned.

A long sought reunion is at hand. You know what to do.

Then, the final song on the mixtape started.

"Just don't go off and—"

"I've got to find him!" Charles launched, shambling in a stupor. "If the stormtroopers catch him, it's going to be interrogation, torture, and God knows what else!"

"Charles, wait!"

He snatched his revolver off the bar, stumbling out the door. Cold air slapped him in the face. The chorus kicked in. This changed everything. If Victor was alive, he would find him.

"Hang in there, buddy," he wheezed. "I'm coming for you.

Running past the opium dens and brothels, Charles leapt up a chain link fence, climbing like a gangly lizard, until he hopped back into Serfdom One. He cracked open the six-shooter, trying to check his ammo in the bad lighting. Three shots. Upon seeing them glisten in the gaslight, Charles's stomach dropped, bravery giving way to fear and dread.

What the fuck am I getting myself into?

As industrial ambiance echoed in the distance, Charles sneaked onward, pretending he was playing through *Metal Gear Solid* for the twenty-third time—in first person—with a real gun. His frenzy became fear. Why had he bought the damn thing anyway? The dealer only half-stocked it, too. Not that Charles knew how to aim it, let alone kill someone.

A siren blared in the distance, driving a shiver down his spine. All color vanished from the streets as the gaslights sizzled off one by one—something out of a silent movie. Even the mixtape ended, leaving Charles alone in the dark.

Wait — what is this? Another surge?

The world was gray and lucid again. Usually this happened when Charles was already passed out drunk. His mind was flooded by a dreamlike haze. Even now he could barely see, groping about in a blinding mist. Passing a display of broken televisions, Charles felt a presence circling him. Footsteps echoed in the dark. He cocked his gun, heart pounding.

Dread flooded his mind.

Then a gloved hand fell over his mouth, followed by the stench of chloroform. Limp as a ragdoll, Charles slumped backwards. He was dragged away, heaved into a truck bed, thrust against—something. It was glass, melting as it caved, numbing his body with sharp tingles, as a monochromatic haze enveloped his mind, spacing out of thought and time.

For behind the screen, only Hell awaited him.

CHAPTER THIRTEEN

Lost in the depths of his sleeping mind, Victor heard the arias of his own composition. The novas of neurons swirled, until the Opera House emerged from the cobalt glow of the void. Such was the cornerstone of cosmos. It was Victor's mental estate in the Waking World, and his sole sanctuary in this gothic realm of madness.

Here, on the carpet, that toy rabbit lay by Victor's side — a totem for a power within. He stood up, holding it by a velveteen arm, and looked about. Amongst the classical murals and violet seats, he saw the Impresario upon the stage before the silver screen, leering like a porcelain puppet in a wheelchair — the soft-spoken master of this sea of souls.

"Have you made your decision, Far Messiah?"

"Why did you bring me back?" Victor asked. "You know my answer's going to be the same. You're right about one thing, though. I can't run away from this world so easily."

"Oh." The Impresario cocked his head. "What makes you say that?"

"I don't need your sarcasm," Victor said, slouching in the center seat. "Let's face it — I'm a prisoner here. A prisoner in my own mind. Trapped in another world and all that. But I'm not going to let them die. Charles and Beatrice are all I have left. I don't care what you say—"

"I believe you misunderstood what I meant," the Impresario interjected. "No one is stopping you from saving them. Perhaps such friends will be your first disciples."

"What do you mean?"

"Consider the epics you so admire," the Impresario said. "The heroes whose images echo into this world. All of them had humble beginnings." His bulging eyes fell upon the toy rabbit. "Even Dante was once an unenlightened poet, lost in a dark wood of error."

The screen flashed with brilliance as the orchestra invisible played a nameless symphony—slow and soft—as a prelude. Victor listened intently, able to see the music in his mind's eye.

"As I said, the power of geist is a psycho-spiritual mask, which you may don to combat the enemy." He chuckled. "You have changed since we've last talked. You are not the same narcissist I awakened. Arrogant though you may be, I sense courage and strength in you. Strength enough to challenge this inner darkness."

Victor opened his eyes, seeing his "other self," Dante Alighieri, projected onto the screen. Such was the Poet of the Spheres, with its Venetian mask and Florentine trench coat, its cotton ears long and drooping as a mirror of Victor's own memories—a weapon of willpower.

"However," the Impresario said, "do not underestimate our opponent."

"The daemons behind the screens," Victor said. "And that serial killer. They're after my friends. I don't know why, and I don't care. But I can't just sit by and do nothing."

He stared at Dante's image, who nodded with silent

approval.

"And so, it finally begins," the Impresario said. "Your conviction may be that of a fool, but perhaps it will blossom into a hero's yet." His voice began to fade. "Regardless, you have taken a first step on the road to maturity...." The Opera House was flooded by the fog of waking thoughts. "And I will be watching you with keen interest."

#

"Victor." There was a firm knock on the door. "Victor, it is time."

In his groggy stupor, Victor woke to the motley ceiling of a motel. The toy rabbit lay on his bare chest, its marble eye staring at him. He glanced at the wall clock.

Six-thirty — it would be dusk. I haven't really slept in almost a day.

"We must leave before the curfew strikes," Thaddeus said, his artificial voice vibrating through the drywall. "You have ten minutes. Do not fall back asleep. If you do, I will know."

The clicking ticks forced him awake. Victor pulled himself upright, legs still sore from the long trek to this district. He turned to the sword cane on the night table, smiling. Victor barely knew how to fence, and chivalric combat was beyond him. And yet, there would come a time when only valor might stand between him and certain death.

Out the cracked window he viewed the dull grayness of a numbered residential quarter beneath the Iron Sky. They were the clustered neighborhoods of Serfdom One — a realm of squat tenements, its alleys dotted with ramshackle shelters and vagabond camps.

And Victor's friends were somewhere in Holy Gothica.

It had been two days since he descended to this dark city. It was an adventure many a young man dreamed of, only to be reminded of its terrifying implications—trapped in another world, with all its glory, and all its horror. A world underpinned by his own thoughts, dreams, and fantasies. He was an anomaly in its metaphysics. An outsider, chosen by weird powers, branded with the Gift of Geist, and thrust into a gauntlet of prophecy and fate. And yet, here he was, an eerie pale-skinned brunette, searching for dear friends.

"Where are we going?" Victor called, voice hoarse and weary. "To Yoshiwara?"

"Indeed," Thaddeus replied. "The 105th await my command. And we shall embark to the darkest of the slums. There, we must gather information regarding...."

Spare me the lecture.

Victor shambled into the water closet, staring into the vanity mirror. Dirty bangs drooped over his eyes, which were baggy and sleep-deprived, and his stubble had grown. After gathering his wits, Victor shambled out the door, wearing the same outfit and trench coat, taking his cane with veiny hands. In the dim hall he was greeted by Thaddeus, masked by his iron respirator.

The inquisitor nodded and led the way. He was proper and polished, jackboots clomping and coattails fluttering. Despite the tubes in his neck and his iron lungs, Thaddeus's mechanical breaths seemed more lively than usual—too chipper for Victor's liking. Even his ebony skin glistened in the flickering light. Towards the lobby, the inquisitor was sure to nag him.

"Recite to me our purpose here," he said.

"Go to the red-light district." Victor felt his way along the peeling wallpaper. "Find out where Leng is, and ask around for Charles's whereabouts too. With any luck, we'll get a lead on the Dollmaker, and then, we go from there."

"And what are we *not* doing?" the Inquisitor asked.

"Give me a chance to wake up."

"What are we not doing, Victor?"

"Associating with harlots," he mumbled. "No hookers and blow."

"Excellent." The inquisitor descended the stairs. "Let us be off."

Victor almost forgot about the stormtroopers of the 105th, waiting for them by the stables outside, all in gas masks and long coats. The counter worker took Thaddeus's payment with shaky hands, desperate to send the inquisitor on his way.

Victor smiled apologetically as they left.

"Ser Thaddeus." Captain Hildegarde rose, donning a freshly shined helmet. "Has your ward recovered at long last? We have much work to do. Yoshiwara awaits my men."

"Indeed," Thaddeus replied. "But we must be careful. I trust you understand, Captain. You and your company must stand by. Your presence will only provoke the masses."

"I see." There was a hint of disapproval in Hildegarde's voice. "Then I shall report to the Empress of our ... 'progress.' I trust she will be quick to reply."

"Pardon?" Thaddeus's brow furrowed. "I know your Men are anxious to see combat. However, as you said, this is an investigation. Not a military operation."

"Understood," the captain replied. "Though my instructions differ, Inquisitor." She drew a crisp envelope from a satchel, stamped with the Corvus Seal. "Perhaps the Empress forgot to mention it, but my men were sent to survey your— investigation." She eyed Victor through soulless goggles. "And our Holy Pontiff has rather low expectations."

Thaddeus did not reply, as if stunned by Hildegarde's disrespect.

"I will rally the troops upon your command, Ser Thaddeus,"

141

the captain said. "However, try not to keep Her Holiness waiting. Time is short."

"I will do what needs to be done." Thaddeus cocked his head, and Victor followed suit. They gave one last look to the six soldiers, who stared back with eerie intent.

They're hiding something.

Traveling on foot, Victor noticed the dirt road gave way to a cobblestone street. He did not recognize the serfdom ahead. It was a far cry from the other ghettos. Haphazard towers rose behind a wall of street art, searchlights shining across the narrows, perched atop a plateau of sewer pipes. The district stood by the reeking water of the River Noir, which ran through the city's aqueducts, filling the boilers of many breweries and factories. Indeed, Victor recognized the kanji-like script and red paper lanterns, guessing where Thaddeus led him.

"Turn away from this village of sin," an evangelist shouted from atop a soapbox. "You will only lose your soul to the harlots within!"

A train of chilled cars whistled past them, rolling from the breweries towards the taverns. Sticking to the uneven sidewalk, Victor followed Thaddeus down the street, pushing past a mob of drunken dandies. They swayed as a mass of top hats and waistcoats. As the people carried on, Victor felt a strange blend of excitement and dread. Even from that threshold, painted like a leering harlequin, he smelled opium smoke and sewage.

Victor looked back. "So, the 105th aren't coming with us?"

"No," Thaddeus replied. "Yoshiwara is not welcoming to the Stormtrooper Corps, let alone anyone who openly supports the Imperium." His mechanical boots clanked against the cobblestones, his breathing ragged and deep. "It is a lawless place."

Past the Grinning Gates, Victor couldn't help but stare

142

at the gangsters. They wore silver and spiked collars, some with trench coats and others sleeveless tops, all embittered by poverty. They were the next generation of Holy Gothica, seeking a life away from the Ecclesiarchy.

Like if Haight Street met the Kowloon Walled City.

Yoshiwara itself was a fusion of east and west—a patchwork quilt of sushi carts, teahouses, and absinthe bars. It was claustrophobic, and its streets were uneven, the lopsided buildings casting a shadow of false joy against scarlet lights. On the horizon, rising above it all, Victor saw a triple-tiered tower of nouveau design, like a spire of carnal desire.

"Ah, the Sunset Pagoda," Thaddeus said. "Leng always brags about the—women of this establishment. Perhaps we can find him there."

Victor looked about. "Why are there no cameras here? This place is still a part of Holy Gothica, right? I mean, there's no curfew, no guardsmen. Nothing."

"Yoshiwara is 'Serfdom Two' in name only," Thaddeus explained. "Lord Montmartre has a fondness for 'evening pleasures,' as do much of the aristocracy above us. They use Yoshiwara as a massive brothel, where the rich can mingle with these—creatures."

"Doesn't that go against everything your church stands for?"

"Yes," Thaddeus said. "The Inquisition has no real power here, and many treat it as a blind spot. A blight of anarchy in our shining church-state. I may call it indecent, but the Empress allows its monopoly to continue, despite the spread of heresy in this district."

As they continued through the alleys, Victor saw posters, all of red and black, depicting a spray-painted legion of ragtag militiamen, led by a faceless bannerman with a hand

outstretched, as if offering a place in a grand rebellion, reading,
JOIN THE EXPLOSIVE TOMORROW
JOIN THE POWDER KEGS

"Powder Kegs?" Victor called. "What are they?"

"I was hoping you wouldn't see that," Thaddeus hissed. "They are a band of political dissidents. A small yet potent insurgency, composed of triads and gangs. Heretics, the lot of them. Their leader, Ser Ludwig, is one of the most wanted persons in Holy Gothica. He is the self-proclaimed, 'King of the Lepers.' His terrorists and renegades are infamous for their bombing runs, waging a civil war from places where my warrants are useless."

"Meaning, you can't just arrest them?"

"By Imperial Law, I cannot even remove those posters," Thaddeus explained. "This place is utterly outside my jurisdiction. And while Yoshiwara may be a haven for hedonism, I like to think it's — pragmatic. To keep the youth under control, if you will."

"Sounds corrupt to me." Victor shoved his hands into his pockets. He tried to act nonchalant, eyes following a woman in a corset. "But it's oddly enchanting, in a—"

"Don't you dare," Thaddeus growled. "You will not associate with these harlots. Find yourself a good woman of faith." His tone lowered. "You deserve better."

Victor smirked, thinking of how Beatrice would react. "I know someone who'd have a field day with you. Back home, that's what we call 'a virgin-whore complex.'"

"Be that as it may, I do not trust this place. Nor anyone in it."

As they passed the "curiosity shops," Victor saw a backwater cemetery and a marble memorial to a most beloved courtesan, its placard reading,

LADY HIMIKO FUKUHARA
Red Lady of Yoshiwara
Deceased, Maitus 2nd, 1884

Victor felt the statue gaze in turn, eyes chiseled in stone. He stepped forward and heard a melody play in the back of his mind—a requiem on strings. Whoever Fukuhara really was, she must have meant a great deal to many people, and her death quite tragic.

"Victor," Thaddeus called. "We are almost there. Come."

As they reached the doorstep of the Sunset Pagoda, the inquisitor halted. "I shall investigate your friends' whereabouts. However, I have a task for you—retrieve Leng for me. I have a feeling he'll respond better to your call than mine."

"What makes you say that?"

"He respects you." Thaddeus turned his back. "I will return in due time. Just promise me you won't try anything foolish, and don't forget we are on official business."

With that, Thaddeus departed. Victor stared at the doorstep, hearing laughter and moans within. In a nearby alley, he saw a familiar caravan, all violet and velvet, reading on its side,

MUNCHAUSEN CANDY CO.
TOYS, TRINKETS, AND MORE

Victor's heart sank, remembering those two chocolatiers, Edgar and Brutus. There was always a broken glimmer in Edgar's eyes as he tossed "goodies and chewies" to the orphans, masking his despair with charity. And as for Brutus, his mind was ravaged by leprosy, reduced to a mere simpleton by years of disease and hardship.

What the hell could they be doing here?

A tingle ran down Victor's spine. The streetlights flashed off, and all turned deathly quiet. His hand fell over the sword— he knew this was a surge. As the fog thickened, the only sound came from a radio by a boarded window. From those speakers Victor heard a familiar voice, distorted by static. He could have sworn it was Charles in the white noise, until the lamps sparked back on and life resumed.

Victor sighed with relief and loosened, but that voice did not leave him. With nothing else left to do, he took a deep breath and plunged into the alluring underworld.

Here it goes.

#

Inside the Sunset Pagoda Victor shuddered, wandering past the voluptuous dancers. He wheezed at the cigarette smoke, watching as thugs and fools drank away their sorrows, betting on tarrochi gambits. Prostitutes cooed over their shoulders, cleavage spilling from their blouses, legs laced in fishnets and thigh-highs, can-can skirts of a dozen and one colors.

Should I be terrified or aroused?

Making his way to the ballroom, Victor beheld a nightclub of throbbing beats and lights, where the Electro-Jazz Orchestra played onstage, flanked by striptease poles and cage dancers. A sea of coats and corsets swayed in tune to its music, lyrics little more than sensual whispers.

Thaddeus would burst an aneurysm if he saw this.

Victor tried to avert his eyes out of some waning sense of modesty. He dove to the west hall, lest he be swept up by the opium-fueled madness. Eventually he came to the "library" and its back bar. It was quieter, but the jazz still reached him. The bookshelves were curved, lined with erotica and poetry, and he saw a familiar figure sitting at a table by his lonesome.

"Edgar?" Victor called. "What are you doing here?"

The chocolatier, wearing the same orange and silver suit, slouched over a bottle of gin as a most pathetic clown. "Huh?" He lifted his head. "Oh, you're that boy from before." He gave

146

a nervous smile. "What brings you here? This is no place for those young at heart."

"I was about to ask you the same thing." Victor's eyes fell upon an open locket by Edgar's hand, with the sepia photo of a beautiful geisha. "Huh, who is that?"

Lady Fukuhara, maybe?

Victor caught a flash of pain in Edgar's eyes. He dashed the locket aside, face twisting from anger to embarrassment. "No one of importance." He eyed a passing dancer. "You are right, this is no place for me either. But I come here to forget. To escape."

Victor saw Brutus slouched at the bottom of a staircase. His jawless mouth was covered by that wooden mask, his cumbersome body robed in his security blanket, staring at Victor with dull, bloodshot eyes. Then he raised a fistful of lollipops, mesmerized by their color.

"Now." Edgar raised an eyebrow. "Where is your inquisitor friend?"

"Thaddeus isn't around," Victor said. "Actually, he sent me here to find Leng."

"Leng—please, don't speak of him." Edgar gritted his teeth, pointing to the billiard room. "If it's that *pervert* you want, he's at the other bar." He shuddered. "I am sorry. There is something else bothering you. What is it?" He tried to smile. "If I can help...."

"Well." Victor kept it short. "I don't suppose you've seen a middle-aged man with long, silver hair around here, maybe recently? Have you?"

Edgar took a long drink. "Can't say I have. Then again, I'm not one to pay attention to such things. You'd best be careful, though. The Dollmaker is still at large." He shuddered. "Please, I've lost someone very dear to me. I trust you understand."

Brutus stood up, towering over the bouncers, walking towards them.

Victor flinched. "I understand. Well, thank you for your time."

As he left, Victor heard Edgar whimpering over that locket, a broken shell of a man. "Who?" he wept, as Brutus laid a bloated hand on his shoulder. "Who in the world could have killed her? All I did was have an affair, and now— It's just too horrible."

Can't help but feel sorry for him.

#

Across the clicking cues of the billiard room, Victor saw Leng laughing to himself. The deputy was disheveled and hunched as usual, dressed in a cheap suit and tie. His yellow raincoat was draped over the counter, that revolver still dangling from his belt.

"Uh...." Victor tapped his shoulder. "Leng?"

"Huh?" He glanced over, hair disheveled. "Victor! Never thought I'd see you down here! Damn! You got balls to come here alone."

"Funny you mention that."

"Pull up a chair, I'll call over the geishas. You haven't lived until you've passed out on a lady's bosom." Leng finished his drink in a single swig. "I'll pay. You need to get laid."

"Leng, seriously," Victor said. "Thaddeus and I need your help."

"Thaddeus." Leng waved his hand. "When does that fucker not need my help? I mean, seriously. He would be excommunicated if I hadn't taken up that job and—wait a second." He flagged the bartender. "Another dripper! This bastard needs to catch up!"

Hang on, is that—absinthe?

The bartender nodded, placing a fountain of emerald liquid on the table. Victor had never tried it before. He'd heard the legends of wormwood, and the fabled exploits of Charles —

"Here you go, kid."

Victor snapped back to the present as Leng shoved a full glass his way. What was that spoon for again? Before Leng could warn him, Victor took a deep gulp, hoping to grasp such bohemian glory. He was mistaken — his tongue was bombarded by half-dissolved sugar and arsine "flavor." It scorched his throat with sickly sweetness. He stifled a gag, pushing the glass aside.

So much for the green fairy.

"It's not for everyone," Leng said. "I'll get you a whiskey sour."

It went on like this for a long while, until he finally lent Victor an ear.

"So." Leng nodded once the story was finished. "You're basically one of us now. I understand, given the circumstances — but Far Messiah? That's a stretch, even for Thaddeus." He bit his lip. "Hey, no offense. I'm just not sure you're a goddamn savior. That's all."

"I'm not sure either." Out of courtesy, Victor finished another shot. "You and Thaddeus are helping me, so I'm helping you. Just don't be surprised if I leave after this."

"Back where you came from? I understand, but— Damn, I think I've had too much."

"Really?" Victor grinned. "I'm surprised you haven't vomited."

"Me too, man." Leng hoisted up another glass. "Here's to not puking everywhere, or some shit." His eyes narrowed, watching Edgar and Brutus shamble out the back door, the former sobbing all the while. "But that's the least of my worries."

149

"That escalated quickly." Victor raised an eyebrow, keeping to his drink.

"You really want to know?" Leng bit his lip. "Well, you're going to find out sooner or later. And I'd rather you hear it from me, not from whichever hooker you wind up with. It's about Fukuhara. You know, the starlet of Yoshiwara — or at least, she *was*."

The jazz seemed quieter now. Victor listened closely.

"Yeah, I was involved with her too." Leng smirked, sadly. "Well, I wouldn't say *actually* involved. It's hard to tell, you know? Whether they want your wallet or your soul." He muttered something under his breath. "Anyway, she was going to quit the business. Trying to be discreet about it. You can tell how well *that* ended."

"A crime of passion?" Victor asked.

"Hell if I know. It must have started that way. Or maybe her killer had some esoteric plan all along, and Fukuhara was just in the wrong place at the wrong time." Leng shook his head. "At least the times we had were pretty good."

"What was it like?" Victor asked. "I mean — "

"Dating a hooker? Unhealthy. That's probably the best way to describe it. You can't trust them." He looked away. "It all starts off fine, sure. A girlfriend you pay to have around. Breaks the ice quick. But once you start to get 'invested,' you question things. After all, how can you believe in someone like that?"

"I guess — "

"I'll tell you how — you *can't*. And I'm not the only one who got hurt." He took a long draw. "For some people, all it takes is one wrong move. And then — well, the oldest profession was never the most civilized. Don't ever forget that."

"How did it end?" Victor asked.

"Who's the interrogator again?" Leng scoffed. "Anyway, I

150

figured out she was working outside of our agreement. Seeing someone I'd told her not to. That's when I decided to cut it off. I just wish I'd stayed a little longer, because—that's when she went missing. Next day, she's impaled on a telephone pole. The Dollmaker's first kill."

Victor looked away. "I'm sorry, Leng."

"Eh, I don't need your sympathies. You're still young and naive." Finally, a smile crossed Leng's face. "Speaking of which, what kind of girls do you like?"

"Excuse me?"

"I know you don't get off from writing music. What's your type?"

Victor took another long sip. "Raven hair. Green eyes, alabaster skin, punky sense of fashion, sardonic, sassy, and sexy—and if she's into it, she'd be a dom, too."

"Heh," Leng chuckled. "Victor's got a kinky side? Well, I guess brains and bondage are two great tastes that taste great together."

"I don't get out much. What about you?"

"Honestly?" Leng's eyes glazed over. "It's complicated. I mean, I dig hookers just as much as the next guy, but...." He stared into his glass. "You know, Victor, this world is going straight to Hell, but what can I really do? I mean, you can't fight fate, right? So, instead of going all Thaddeus and lying to myself, I just do what I want."

"Why did you join him?" Victor asked. "You clearly don't believe in all this."

"So I could carry a gun." Leng fondled his revolver until his eyes met with Victor's. "Come on, can you really blame me? I'm surprised you haven't gotten shot yet! And to be honest, the whole 'deathly afraid of blood' thing is just good acting. I'm not afraid to fake sick, if it means I don't have to butcher people.

Used to act in my own films, actually."

"I see," Victor said. "Also, I'm here for another reason."

"Oh?" Leng raised an eyebrow.

"Two friends of mine. You know. They arrived here apparently a month before me. Beatrice and Charles. Have you heard anything about them, down here?"

"Huh." Leng's brow furrowed. "The name 'Charles' rings a bell. I might have gone drinking with him before. Tall, middle-aged, glasses, kinda odd like you—"

"That's him. How did you know?"

"I meet a lot of destitutes down here." Leng pushed his shot glass aside. "Just another low-level bureaucrat drowning his sorrows in gin. Sad. No one should have to resort to gin. Anyway, I don't know where he is exactly." His smile widened. "But someone else might."

"I'm not going to end up cockfighting or something, am I?"

"Not in the way you're thinking, no," Leng chuckled. "Yuko. Third floor. Room 336."

"Wait." Victor's stomach plummeted. "Are you setting me up with a—harlot?"

"Catching on quick, aren't we? Seriously. If it took you that much to loosen up, you *really* need to get laid. And don't call them harlots. You sound like Thaddeus. They prefer 'courtesan' or 'mistress.' Yuko's the latter. If you're into that."

"No." Even plastered, Victor had some vestige of his principals. "I can't sleep with a prostitute, even if it means not finding my friends. That's just *wrong*."

"Who says you have to sleep with her? You don't have to— it's just a huge plus, in my opinion. Seriously, I'm sure she'll tell you anything you want to hear."

"All right, I guess."

"I'll let her know. Just knock three times, she'll say come

in—you know the drill." With that, Leng got up and staggered towards the ballroom. "Anyway, I gotta piss. Have fun!"

The inquisitor vanished down the hall into the howling crowd. For now, Victor was alone with half a fountain of absinthe, and his own thoughts.

Well, shit.

CHAPTER FOURTEEN

"Never waste booze, Victor. It's not about being manly, it's about *etiquette*."

Such had been Charles's worldly advice on Victor's twenty-first birthday. The hangover begged to differ, but the moral stuck to this day. Meanwhile, in the Sunset Pagoda, a good hour passed as Victor sipped at the final drops of absinthe, until he slid the glass across the bar, laying his head in his hands. His mind was numb, save for the memory of why he was there.

I really should be searching.

Slowly he phased out of consciousness, feeling the cool bar against his flushed cheeks. All was a swimming sea of darkness and starlight, until he drifted into slumber.

Victor remembered it. The day he and Charles first met.

It had been three years ago in the Waking World, when the carnival came to town. And it was already dusk when Victor and a few acquaintances decided to pay the twenty-dollar fee. Naturally, he protested against such a prospect. It was like not going to prom, only justifiable. It was all flickering lights and rickety rides, complete with the discord of pubescent voices.

I could be composing right now.

Sponsored by what money the high schools had left over, the carnival rolled from the rural tracks to the north side of town. Victor strayed from the group, which was already headed towards the "food court." Hands shoved deep into his pockets, Victor wandered about, greasy bangs covering his acne-blasted brow, flexing the overdeveloped muscle on his neck.

I don't even know anyone here. All from different schools.

Eventually he came to the blue portables. No one was there, probably because of the smell. Victor didn't really care. Leaning against a wall, he sighed, kicking dust off a plank of wood, watching the sun go down, feeling the same dread from when he was a child, and —

"Damn punks," someone hissed. "They don't pay me enough for this."

Victor spun around, half-expecting some strongman to come around with a hammer, only to see a middle-aged man in a chicken suit, wiping the sweat off his brow, adjusting his tea shades. His eyes fell on Victor, and he tried to muster a smile.

"Oh, hey," he said. "Another gloomy ball of angst. S'up?"

Victor didn't say anything, going back to his brooding.

The man was about to walk away. "Hope you're having fun by not having fun, because we don't do refunds." He smiled. "Can you imagine that? We'd be out of business!"

Victor bit his lip, trying not to laugh. Almost keeping composure for some imaginary goth girl staring him in the face, as if he would get a blowjob for acting cool and aloof.

"Hang on." The man turned around, eyes widening. "Did you just — ?"

"What?"

"You were totally smiling for a second! Not smirking. *Smiling*." He crossed those feathery arms. "I'm kind of proud of myself." He pulled out a spliff from behind his ear and lit it.

155

"Gotta say, not every day that happens. There's a reason I'm off clown duty."

"Is a walking cock a step up or down?"

"Oof." The man rolled his eyes, clutching his chest. "Right in the dignity." He sighed. "Don't worry, kid. I actually prefer it. Same reason you wear your hair like that."

"Huh?" Victor brushed away his oily bangs. "What do you mean?"

"I can't stand people either." The man sighed, taking a puff of his joint. "This suit is actually a shield. Something I put on a show with, something to hide myself in. So I don't get hurt. I wear this like a knight in armor. It's a part of me, but not all of me. Like how you put on the goth act, when really, you're a nerd." He blew a smoke ring. "You're in school, right?"

"High school, yeah." Victor shrugged. "Creepy question, though. Why?"

"Nah, thought you were a freshman in college. Too many young people wasting away their lives, like me." His smile turned bittersweet. "Sorry, I kinda ramble."

"I do the same thing."

"But yeah." Charles nodded. "That's why I'm heading back to college this fall. Scholarships for burners exist. Imagine that." He turned to the Ferris wheel. "But tonight's my last night as a carnie. Thank God. Soon, I'll be a forty-year-old student."

It was getting dark, but for once, Victor felt at ease.

"What's your name?" He stepped forward. "I'm Victor."

"Charles Garner." The man outstretched a hand. "Nice to meet you."

"I'll be there next fall too." Victor shook it, trying to ignore the reek of cannabis. "Guess I might see you around in a few months?"

"Yeah, you don't seem like a little shit. I'll say hey." Charles turned his back, walking towards the light fixtures. "Well, my break's over. Come by the freak show if you wanna chat!"

And they would for a long while.

"You okay?" A gruff voice penetrated his stupor. "Hey, kid. No passing out at the bar."

"S-sorry." Victor's eyes rolled open, back to Holy Gothica. "I'm fine."

The billiard room was starting to close down, the lights dimming, as wheeled labori came with brooms and mops, shaped like oversized trash cans.

"You sure?" The bartender stared him in the face. "If I had a copper for each time youngsters came here and drank themselves to hell and back—well, I wouldn't be tending." He gave a throaty chuckle. "I think you better cut yourself off. Last call, anyway."

"You might be right," Victor slurred, remembering why he was there.

"Well, here you go." The bartender slid him a brass key. "The third floor is exclusive to our favorite patrons. Leng's one of them, and he insisted on paying on your behalf."

"Oh." Victor took the key with drooping fingers. "Thanks."

"No trouble, all right?" The bartender raised an eyebrow. "I don't want no foul play."

Realizing there was no way around this, Victor thought it best to face what he needed to do. He shambled up the many flights of stairs and came to the top tier of the Sunset Pagoda. He braced himself for the worst, staring at the door to Room 336, knuckles white and hands shaking, until he knocked thrice on the door. And yet, Victor couldn't help but smile at it all.

Charles — if only you could see me now.

157

CHAPTER FIFTEEN

Victor shifted his boots. He was tempted to knock again, but thought better of it. Adjusting his coat's collar, he scanned the hallway, seeing a framed poster on the wall with the image of a copper android, much like the ones downstairs.

NO HEART. NO SOUL. NO SALVATION.

For a moment, Victor pondered the labori and their role in this society. They probably formed the backbone of Holy Gothica's industrial powerhouse. People who saw them as artificial intelligences were no doubt heretics. As for where Victor fell on such matters, he had never given it much thought, besides in philosophy classes and cyberpunk milieu.

Like the Chinese Room theory. Or Blade Runner.

When the door opened, Victor stared, awestruck. Yuko's flowing locks of scarlet hair shimmered in the lamplight, eyes glistening like emeralds. Dressed in a see-through kimono of black lace, with a corset and lingerie underneath, she beckoned him into her chamber.

Wait. Are those stitches or rivets?

158

As she turned around to grab a bottle of sake, Victor saw that the back of her corset was not lacing at all. They were cables. And yet, Victor thought he recognized her from somewhere. Her eyes were fluorescent, the corners of her mouth stitched like a ragdoll's smile—calm and gentle, far from hollow, yet nonetheless artificial. She was a pinup model out of a seamstress's fever dream. As Victor felt the blood rush to his cheeks, he recalled numerous fantasies and fetishes long repressed.

Did Leng just buy me a night with a sexbot?

"Victor, right?" Her voice was oddly human. "Leng let me know you were coming."

He nodded, taking a few steps, catching the wafting scent of jasmine. It was a room of reds, violets, and velvets. With a huge heart-shaped bed that could easily hold four people, and no doubt had, the chamber was spotted with all manner of kinky toys, ranging from whips and wax, to chains and collars. But what troubled Victor most of all was the bulge in his slacks.

"You're from the City Above, aren't you?" Yuko's ruby lips curled into a soft smile. "Can I interest you in some refreshment? You seem like you want to savor this."

Victor nodded—a few more drinks were called for.

Yuko poured two glasses of rice wine, sitting on the bed. "Don't be shy."

He took a deep breath and sat on the far edge, feeling his face turn a deeper shade of red.

She handed Victor the fuller glass. "So, what do you want exactly?"

"Nothing, really." He managed to choke. "Just p-passing through—"

"Really?" Yuko scoffed. "If we're going to have any fun, you might as well loosen up a bit." Her bangs covered only one eye, giving her a "femme fatale" look. She stroked Victor's cheek with a smooth hand. He shuddered, avoiding eye contact. "Now, what brings you here?"

Victor finished the contents of his glass swiftly. "G-good stuff." He tried to change the subject. "Yeah, well, to be honest, I came here to hide, and — find some answers."

"So, you're on the run?"

"Not really to hide." Victor pondered for a moment. "Well, yes, b—but—"

"I'm just teasing you." The courtesan moved closer. "Also, if it's finances that's got you worried, don't bother. Leng already paid for you."

Victor's eyes wandered about the room, from the baroque mirrors, to bookshelves lined with the occult and weird tales. He tried to distract his libido, out of some semblance of "chivalry," or whatever tact he could muster.

What the — ?

The next thing he knew Yuko was atop him, unbuttoning his shirt, staring him mischievously in the eye, rocking her hips over his, nipples puckering behind a slipping bra.

"I take it this is your first time."

"Really." Victor scoffed. "Did Leng tell you that? O-oh.... Oh my...."

Victor's eyes rolled back. Her hands caressed his chest, moving towards his manhood. But two things perplexed Victor, despite his intoxication and allurement. The first was that the model seemed sentient. Either that or she could fake emotion disturbingly well. She was a machine after all, and as awesome as this Industrial Revolution was, could it really create a living, feeling computer? Still, she was obviously not some factory tool—she was human unless one looked close enough. If she could dream and feel as humans did, then what

160

did her kind endure? They were household slaves at best, and outright fodder at worst.

Victor shuddered to think if these models could feel pain.

But he did not know what to conclude—the trend could be swayed either way. But then, other questions nagged at the back of his mind. Just what was this woman's story? What drove her to prostitution? Who was she? Beautiful as she was, Victor felt more pity than arousal.

"Hey." Yuko stroked his cheek. "Are you all right? You're a little limp."

"I c-can't...."

"Are you sure?" Yuko frowned. "This is already paid for."

"Well, y-you're a—you know." Victor stared at her. "Can you think?"

She gave a soft laugh. "I can think and feel just as well as you can, contrary to popular belief. That's not to say I have rights, though." She stared at him. "But seriously? *That's* what's cockblocking you?"

"Do you have a soul?" Victor was just as harrowed as he was curious. "I mean, can machines make music? That's what I meant."

"You know, some people get straight to the point," she smiled, sharp yet genuine. "It sounds like you're asking me if I dream of clockwork sheep. But, let me ask *you* a question. Let's say machines made men, hypothetically—would that change things?"

"I suppose not."

"Yeah, I believe that being artificial, or even alive, has nothing to do with emotion or thought. It's a matter of cognition. The ability to process and learn."

"You're very logical. I can't argue that," he said.

"All good philosophy comes down to logic. Anyway, how

do you like it?"

"Okay." Victor slapped a palm to his face. "Look, I didn't know that this was part of the deal. I just wanted to find out where one of my friends, one of your customers, is. I had no idea that this was involved. Well, I did—that's a blatant lie. You're damn gorgeous and all. Don't get me wrong. It's just I can't help but feel like I'm taking advantage of you. That's it."

Yuko gave an honest smile. "That might be the most genuine thing a customer has ever said to me. Can't say I'm not a bit sad, though. Compared to some of the sleazebags I've had, you're pretty cute, in that wallflower sort of way."

"T-thanks."

Sitting on the edge of the bed, Victor relaxed and talked to Yuko. As his stupor lingered, he told her about his misadventures from the beginning. Maybe it was the liquor, but she seemed trustworthy. A person he could open up to. Regardless, he made sure to mention Charles and Beatrice on multiple occasions, insisting on finding their whereabouts.

"Damn," she interjected. "That all happened in two days?"

"Yeah," Victor sighed. "Like I said, I have no idea what's going on. All I know is that Thaddeus thinks I'm some kind of messiah." He paused. "I shouldn't have said that. Anyway, about my friends. We think they're here in Yoshiwara. Do you know anything?"

"Charles? I think I met him once. Middle-aged guy, right? Long gray hair? Glasses? Yeah, he was a lot like you, in the way that he backed out. And then he started crying." Yuko looked away. "Come to think of it, he did mention a 'brother from another mother.'"

"T-that's him." Victor couldn't help but smile. He stared out the window at the dimming gaslights—maybe he would find Charles again. "Yeah, that's him."

Yuko nodded thoughtfully. "I'd just be careful if I were you."

"I've been getting that a lot."

"No, really." Yuko looked him in the eye. "Yoshiwara isn't some anarchic utopia. In fact, it's about as far as from that you can get. Between the triads and gangs, not to mention what they put in the absinthe, this place is dangerous as all hell. What's your plan anyway? It sounds like you're just wandering around till you get shot. You can stay a while if you want."

"I appreciate it." Victor smiled. "But this is something I have to do."

She stood up. "Well, if I can't stop you, I might as well help. You clearly came here for information — something Leng conveniently forgot to mention. What else do you want to know?"

Victor considered his possible questions. "Well, what do you know about the killer?"

"Most of his targets are prostitutes." Yuko's face turned grim. "They all go missing just before a surge hits, too. Weirdest part is, they don't always have a customer. And ever since the killings started, so did all this supernatural shit. The downtrodden are just fuel for the fire."

"That's disturbing."

"You're telling me," Yuko said. "Not to mention, they are always found impaled on telephone poles, drained of their blood. Like they're being fed to a swarm of leeches." There was a glimmer of fear in her eyes. "Why blood, though? I really don't know. They sure as fuck aren't virgins, so eternal youth is out of the question." She chuckled bitterly. "Still, the bastard is getting off on this. And the stormtroopers couldn't care less."

Victor looked away, tantalized by her perfume.

"Anyway," she said, "your 'guides' probably won't be back

for a while. You can stay the night if you want." Her lips curled into a coy smile. "Free of charge."

"Can we make it platonic?" Victor blurted.

"I've done weirder things than be a cuddle-buddy."

#

When Yuko shut off the lights, Victor lay awake for a long while. Between a woman's touch and the ticking clock, it was impossible to sleep. Brushing her aside, Victor staggered up, still a little drunk. Then he glanced at the television on a vanity shelf.

On the other side was Victor's reflection, warped by its convex screen. Feeling the blood rush to his head, Victor turned away, seeing a bookshelf, laden with a number of philosophical texts. One in particular caught his eye, titled, *OF CARDINAL SIN*.

Picking up the musty book, he flipped to a random passage, reading,

As a green-eyed leviathan, the Sin of Envy swallows all it desires, robbing one's neighbors of happiness, and one's self of kindness. It is the maelstrom of pettiness, seeking to fill its yawning void, but nothing shall ever be enough. Indeed, Envy is the corrupted want for what one's fellow man possesses, be it physical or spiritual, whether by spite or misfortune. And like all of sin, it is only through divine submission that one may overcome it, or else, be consumed by the daemons that so revere its gaze.

Victor yawned. Such tirades always bored him. He shut the book, having had enough of religious horror for one night, until he heard the television buzz on.

He hadn't touched the remote.

When Victor looked back the suite had darkened, save for

164

that screen, tuned to a dead channel, speakers buzzing with white noise. He reached for his sword cane that was propped against the nightstand, expecting a horde of daemons to come crawling forth—and yet, something could be seen beyond that haze. A man was trapped behind the screen, writhing. Although the droning grew louder, Victor heard a familiar voice beyond its pulsing base.

"Charles? Is that—?" He tripped over his own feet. "Shit!"

Catching himself on the television, Victor's hand slapped against its screen. But as his knuckle dug into the glass, it rippled into a dark portal. His forearm plunged into whatever lay beyond, numbed by a tingling sensation. Something thick and wet grappled him, like a tentacle of roiling ooze. Shocked, Victor struggled with all his strength until he somehow broke free, slamming his head against the bed as the television flashed off.

"What the *hell*?" Yuko jerked awake. "Victor, are you okay?"

"I...." He tried to speak past the aches, his worst fears realized. "I....!"

She turned on the light, but terror did not leave him. Victor saw what he saw, and knew what it meant. Charles had been taken by the Dollmaker, trapped inside whatever that place was. He was at the mercy of daemons now. It was probably only a matter of time before he wound up dead. Or maybe he was already impaled on a telephone pole, waiting to be discovered.

Then a pair of jackboots stomped up the stairs.

"In the name of all things holy, why?!" A familiar voice boomed down the hall. "You have some *damn* good explaining to do, Leng!"

"Heh, I think that's the first time I've heard you swear!"

Yuko leapt up, drawing a revolver from under her pillow.

165

"Who the hell is that?!"

Victor tried to speak, but no words came. He cradled his skull, trying to suppress his panic. His breathing grew rapid, his eyes twitched. Standing up with shaky knees, he tried to draw himself away from the screen but couldn't, out of fear.

"Attention, Yuko!" A metal fist slammed on the door. "We are agents of Her Holiness's Inquisition! I demand you open this door and surrender your hostage from bondage!"

"Hostage?" Leng cackled. "Holy shit, Thaddeus, he's just getting laid!"

"We don't have time for this," the inquisitor roared. "Quickly, break it down!"

Then Yuko jerked open the door, seeing Thaddeus clutching his sword's hilt.

"I thought I told you," the inquisitor's voice quivered with rage, marching into the room, towards Victor, "not to forget that we are on *official* business. Whatever happened to — ?"

There was a steely click.

"I'm sorry," Yuko growled, pointing her revolver at Thaddeus. "Do you have a *warrant*?"

"Do not test me, woman," Thaddeus said, undeterred. "You are meddling in Inquisitorial affairs, and have waylaid my ward with your siren's song."

"Let me repeat the question."

Their escalation bounced off Victor's ears until Leng came forward. "Hang on, did something happen? Why are you staring like that, Victor? Are you okay?"

Yuko lowered her revolver, turning to Victor. "Wait, you two are with *him*?"

"I saw Charles," Victor choked, heart pounding. "He's — he's...."

Thaddeus turned his attention to Leng, pointing a finger.

"Explain your intent. *Now*."

Leng raised his hands. "I just thought I'd hook Victor up. He wanted to find some information, so I sent him to Yuko. Not that hard to understand." He held back a bashful smile. "I do admit, I was a bit plastered. Give him some credit, though. After all, if he lasted that long with Yuko...." He shot Victor a grin. "Well done, man."

"I'm right here." Yuko rolled her eyes. "Way to warn me, though."

Thaddeus looked about the suite, brow furrowing with utter disgust. "And I take it you are the machine-harlot," he hissed. "You are this 'Yuko?'"

"Yeah, so?" Yuko crossed her arms. "You'll be pleased to hear that Victor is the most prudish customer I've ever had. Not that it's a feat or anything."

"I just c-came for information," Victor managed. "Really."

It took a moment, but Thaddeus seemed to fetter his rage. "Information, you say? And what, pray tell, did you uncover, Victor?" He drew a wrinkled envelope. "For I found this on the fringe of Munchausen Industries, just outside Yoshiwara. I suggest you read it."

Just like the letter from the schoolyard, it was addressed to Victor. With trembling hands, he saw the word, "INVIDIA," printed on the envelope. The font was typed in courier and evenly spaced, yet the crimson ink had bled through the page, carrying a coppery smell.

Victor read it, aloud.

Dear Victor,

I caught wind that your powers have awakened. Splendid! You'll need those. However, two others descended before you, evading my friends for quite some time. This is where the fun begins, I assure you, as I am no longer content with the bloodborne fuel of whores. I'll make it quick, so even the fool at your heels can understand.

Charles is mine, and I shall extract his vitae soon enough.

Vitae is such a beautiful word, don't you think? A beautiful word for a beautiful thing. The mind made material, in all its sin. Such a pity that its harvesting requires such savage deeds. No matter, I shall incubate it within him, sustaining it with madness. But if you want to save him, I'll give you a clue. Look to the train graveyards and the backside of the televisions – Hell is waiting for you.

Just know, after the Devil's Hour, there might not be a friend to find.

Regards,
The Dollmaker

"It is clear now." Thaddeus's eyes widened. "The Dollmaker is using the televisions as his modus operandi. When a surge hits, he throws a wayward soul through the rupturing portal. The daemons are being *fed* by him. And Charles is the next victim." He turned to Victor. "As for the 'backside of the televisions,' he is referring to something we long fought to keep secret."

"Oh, shit." Leng's jaw dropped. "You don't mean the Inferno?"

"I-inferno?" Victor stuttered. "W-what is that?"

"Uh." Leng rubbed his head. "You know, I'm not quite as pious as Thaddeus, but...." He glanced about nervously. "Well, I shouldn't have even said its name."

"The Inferno is something we try to keep hidden from the populace," Thaddeus explained. "But I will not lie to you, Victor. All faith aside, it is where the Cacophony infiltrates our reality. I suspect Charles is trapped in that eldritch place."

"And 'after the Devil's Hour?'" Victor asked. "That means, he'll be killed when the next surge ends, right?" His stomach plummeted. "Assuming he's not already dead."

Thaddeus's silence was not reassuring.

"Wait," Leng said. "The Inferno would channel the sins and repressed thoughts of whoever's trapped inside it, like a self-sustaining torture room. You don't mean—"

"I mean exactly that," Thaddeus interrupted. "Somehow, Charles was forced into the abyss. Trapped in its mist bound prison." A circus tune echoed in the distance, sending shivers down everyone's spines. "Such an environment can only nurture the vitae, ripening it."

Vitae. 'Bloodborne soulstuff.' What the daemons are collecting.

Victor was overcome by dizziness. "W-what's he using the vitae for?"

"That I do not know." Thaddeus looked away. "But it cannot be for anything good. I advise you follow us, Victor. And, as much as it pains me to say it, perhaps Doctor Murdoch is behind it all. Come." He cocked his head. "We must be off. Now."

With that, Thaddeus marched down the hall, back towards the foyer and the gambling halls. Victor felt the weight of Charles's life on his shoulders.

"Hey." Yuko placed a hand on Victor's arm. "You don't look too good. Just remember, if you ever need a place to hide out, Yoshiwara is a haven for misfits like us."

"Thanks, but I'm fine."

"Right." Leng leaned in the doorway. "Things are only going to get worse from here on out. But mark my words, the Dollmaker's gonna pay yet."

"Leng," Thaddeus barked, "quit stalling. I've had enough of this carnal cesspool." His footsteps faded down the hall as he muttered all the while.

"I'll buy you some time." Leng winked. "Who knows when

you'll see *her* again."

The inquisitor winked, closing the door.

"So," Yuko said. "You seem sobered up."

"Not in the mood, really. But—"

Before he knew it, Victor felt Yuko's soft lips pressed against his, however briefly. She tasted like raspberries and dark chocolate, and he all but melted. With a flick of her tongue Yuko parted, fixing her gaze onto Victor's eyes, paralyzing him with fearful desire.

Victor tried to soothe his pounding heart. "I—I have to go."

"Oh, I know." Yuko smiled, coyly. "I'm *letting* you."

CHAPTER SIXTEEN

When Charles awoke, he felt like a corpse adrift at sea. He smelled the hot air, the smog of the city. Only boundless. Endless. Trapped between miasma and buzzing static, behind the screens.

Is this....Hell?

He'd heard rumors of this pale void; the otherworld born from the collective will of man, projected through an industrial lens and filter. Hazy and surreal. And yet, Charles felt the firmness of his own mortality — a lethal dream. He shut his eyes for a moment, and when he opened them, a dark, inner world materialized out of the fog.

No, I remember. Wait, am I inside the TV?

It was a labyrinthine studio, complete with lattice works and set-pieces out of expressionist films, as if this entire place was the backstage of Holy Gothica. A disturbing notion. As giant lamps swayed in the mist, Charles felt a tingle of fear run down his spine. He saw something across the long way — a tower of eternal darkness, with neither summit nor bottom, shrouded in fog, its true form yet unseen.

He stood in limbo before that outermost wall. For here, all

the world was a stage, and yet Charles carried on, squinting past the burning smog, into this "dark wood of error."

Then, he saw what form it took.

Is that a circus? That's just not right.

Beyond its blank gates, big tops and Ferris wheels were visible from the courtyard, looming over lesser tents, all striped with vibrant reds and pitch blacks. The calliope music was menacing, and the attractions gave off an eerie light. It reminded Charles of all those awful gigs he used to get. Worst was the smell, bringing back memories of locker rooms, and upon arriving at its ticket booth, he knew dread, its sign reading in gilded font,

CIRQUE DU CHARLEMAGNE

He forced himself to walk past the yawning gates, down the old railroad. Alongside the rickety rides he was alone in the dark, with nowhere to go but forward. It all smelled like fetid flesh and cannabis, blood and bullet holes scattered about, patterned as unfinished peace signs. And yet no one was there, not even the circus freaks, and that harrowed Charles most of all.

The last thing I need — creepy-ass clowns.

He shuddered, reaching for his revolver. Clowns always made him uneasy—disturbing, uncanny, and just not that funny. As a comedian he respected slapstick, but clowns just tried too hard, as if they were hiding something. He'd had to work with them, back in those amusement park days, and that didn't help anything. Regardless, Charles stood on a railroad track, staring at the logo on a food cart—a smiling pig slicing itself into salami — and he paled.

Just then, a fiendish laugh, not unlike his, echoed on the hot, dry wind.

Charles spun around and wasted a ringing shot. Nothing

was there, but if he carried on like this, something would be. Sure enough, a gang of gating shadows emerged. Charles stumbled backwards and ducked down an alley, clutching his revolver.

Go away…go away…go the fuck away.

As they shambled into the floodlight, Charles had to cover his mouth to keep from screaming. They were miserable things of frilled collars and doll masks, wan flesh glistening with tarrish ooze, arms ending in fists of mechanical claws.

"Jesus Christ!" He cocked his revolver, holding it with both hands. "D-don't come near me!" His grip wavered. "S-stand back! I'll s-shoot you!"

The clowns bounded forward as one swung a blade above its head. Charles flinched and pulled the trigger. There was a crack, and a deafening blast of gun smoke; the recoil slapped Charles in the face, splashed by black blood. A cruel cackle filled the air, but he stood his ground, and the clowns only stared him down with vacant smiles.

Still alive?! How?! Wait – are these daemons?!

Charles saw more of the freaks encroaching from every tent and alley, slithering puddles of ichor, cowled strongmen with bloodstained hammers, firebreathers immolated by their own flames, all masked and laughing mad. Then Charles felt something just behind him. He turned around, seeing his shadow on a train car, moving on its own.

His stomach dropped. "Oh, shit."

It transfigured into a corpse-like mockery of *himself* – eyes replaced by empty voids, its body rippling like the static which birthed it. Gaudy and garish, it was dressed like a gentleman, green and bedazzling, as "a man of wealth and taste." Its face was cracked porcelain, painted like a deranged jester – a younger Charles through a broken mirror of despair and envy.

<del>173</del>

"Pleased to meet you," it said. "Hope you can guess *my* name."

Charles stared, slack-jawed and horrified. "Wait, I.... I...." He stared at the doppelganger's face. "Why do you look like me? W-what the—?"

"What did you honestly expect, dude?" The other Charles stepped forward. "Repressed emotions can bite you hard in the ass." It leaned on a striped cane ending with a jester's head. "It's a little late to dwell on looks, seeing how many chances you passed up for the comfortable road. The easy road. That's why you're here. Looking for Victor?" It outstretched its arms, grinning widely. "Let's face it, you just want to be the hero for once. But in this steampunk shithole, you can't even have that! Not that you even deserve it."

"W-what did you just say?" Charles stepped forward, fists clenched. "It's not like that! I'm doing this for my friend, even if it means— Well, yeah, some recognition would be nice, I admit that. But hey, fuck you!" His eyes narrowed. "What are *you*?"

"I thought I told *you*," the other Charles grimaced. "I'm what you keep locked—but now, I got let loose. And damn, it feels good to be free. I'm a daemon. *Your* daemon." It ran its fingers through its long, blond hair. "And honestly, dude? Instead of looking for Victor, you better start looking for yourself. But then again, what's there to find? You got beat up through high school, your prom date cheated on you with that jock. After that, you *tried* college."

"I went back!" Charles snapped. "And I'm still enrolled, dammit! Stop it! Shut up!"

"Tell that to the twenty plus years you spent wandering the coast," the other Charles sighed. "You drifted from job to job, trying to act like a bohemian. In reality, we both know what you are—a joke. I don't even need to tell you that. You know it. Besides, why else would you go back to school? Even with Victor, you're second fiddle! He's the closest thing to a friend you had. Only because he's too damn autistic to realize what a failure you are—"

"Shut. Up," Charles hissed, fighting back tears. "You leave him out of this, before I—"

"Sticking up for the *retard*? I call bullshit," the other Charles cackled. "You keep him around like a three-legged puppy to make yourself feel better. Deep down you're damn jealous. He has so much potential, something you *never* had."

Charles winced, a hand falling on his revolver.

"Playing tough?" The other Charles said. "You're using him as a crutch, because all you do is crack jokes and smoke weed. But hey, maybe finding your 'friend' can fix that!" Its grin widened to an uncanny degree. "Yeah, right. We both know you're already deader than disco inside. Not that it'll matter soon."

"Y-you...you...!" Charles's voice rose to scream and he opened fire, just twice, until he heard only hollow clicks. The fog of denial blinded the way forward, and he slumped to his knees. "Y-you're wrong! You're not me.... You're *not* me! G-go fuck yourself."

"Heh." The inner daemon pressed cold steel against Charles's forehead. "Whatever. Keeping lying to yourself. Keep turning your head until your darkness grows. After all, 'it's not easy facing up, when your whole world is black!'"

The other Charles jerked his hand upward and pulled the trigger, vanishing as a wisp of gun smoke. As he winced, the lights of a daemon train flashed upon Charles, a hellish roar echoing from its boilers. It rushed towards him at full speed. Before he could even move it smashed into Charles with ethereal force, knocking him flat on his back.

175

Victor....

He was not dead—not yet. Inky tentacles rose from the bottom of the engine, dragging Charles aboard its cars, as the train departed along the tracks, into the mist bound infinity.

I'm sorry. So sorry....

CHAPTER SEVENTEEN

Victor's brow furrowed with worry. The glamour of Yoshiwara was far behind, and he was welcomed back by the bleak apartments of the residential quarters. The stormtroopers of the 105th stood vigil in the distance, saluting Thaddeus and Leng with grim respect, save their captain. Victor couldn't help but notice the civilians passing by, turning their heads, hurrying along with urgency. He shoved his hands deep in his pockets, following Thaddeus's lead.

"Five hours," Captain Hildegarde said. "You were gone for *five* hours."

"I apologize for the inconvenience," Thaddeus replied, trying to mask the spite in his voice. "There were certain matters that needed my attention. At any rate, we have a heading."

And so, Thaddeus relayed his findings to the stormtroopers, emphasizing the potential of another victim should they fail to act. Meanwhile, Victor sat on a rusty bench, laying his head in his hands. He barely noticed Leng, a concerned look on the deputy's face.

Charles. Please, hang in there. Just, stay alive. I'm coming.

"As you can see," Thaddeus concluded. "We must strike

with great vengeance. After all, that is why the Empress sent you gentlemen to assist me."

"I should certainly hope so. Time is short. However," the captain said, glancing at Victor, "the Empress questions your choice in entourage. Field experience I can understand, but...." She stepped forward. "Is there something you are not telling us, Ser Thaddeus?"

Victor stared on. Clouds of moths gathered around the streetlamps.

"Certain details of the investigation are classified," Thaddeus admitted. "And they are no concern of yours. Tell me, though. Are these the Empress's thoughts, or *yours*?"

"Both," the captain said. "And if you wish to regain the Empress's favor, I suggest you cease playing this game of intrigue. It is for your own good — "

"Your chain of command does not concern the mission," Thaddeus barked. "The Empress sent you to assist me. Now, let us carry out our duties. An innocent life is at stake."

Victor raised his head, feeling Leng's hand on his shoulder.

"Hey." The inquisitor tried to smile. "We should get a move on."

The captain gestured, sending a guardsman to the rickety stables. He returned with a pair of hairless horses. As the rest of the soldiers went to mount their steeds, Victor and the inquisitors were left to their own devices. He dreaded riding that gangly steed again.

"They don't trust us," Leng said. "They probably know something's up with Victor."

"I have told no one of my suspicions of divinity, save the Ecclesiarchs." Thaddeus adjusted the brim of his hat. "More than that, the Empress's faith in me is waning. I am merely doing my duty, but...." He looked away. "Something else is at work here."

Victor knew better than to comment.

#

The second journey to the Leper Quarter was long and grim. Victor did not recognize the path they took. The company traveled on horseback, following the River Noir upstream, along its sludge and black shores, staying on the main roads. Even Thaddeus was on edge, keeping a hand on his blessed charms. The stormtroopers kept their halberds and rifles at the ready as strange noises echoed all too near from the lopsided shacks and aqueducts.

"Gentlemen," Thaddeus called. "This spot is well-lit and vacant. Let us rest here."

Victor dismounted his Clydesdale, feeling its skin stretched over a skeletal frame as broken flagstones shifted under his boots. The stormtroopers ignited a campfire out of wooden scraps, huddling around the flames, muttering to one another in military jargon.

One stood away from his band of brothers, reading a tattered primer.

Staring at the soldier under gaslight, Victor noticed how delicately he turned the pages. In between a few leaves, flowers were dried and pressed, and the trooper gazed at them longingly. Victor suspected these faceless soldiers were not so soulless. The stormtrooper glanced at him, snapped the book shut, and stood up, clutching his rifle, as if standing guard. Regardless, this made Victor think about the troopers—if they really were brutal tools of war at heart. For war brings out the worst in men, but does it omit the good?

Perhaps it was just harder to see at times, but still....

"Don't be so glum." Leng sat beside him. "We're almost there."

"That's what I'm afraid of."

Leng took a swig from his flask. "That means you're not stupid. But, just out of curiosity, why did you join Thaddeus? I doubt it was for faith and duty." He offered Victor a drink. "It's all about your friends, isn't it? You think they're out there. Alive."

"I can still hope." Victor took a sip; it smelled like rat piss. He gagged, handing back the flask. "How can you drink that?"

"It's an acquired taste." Leng took another gulp. "Like working for the Imperium. Anyway, about your friends. Don't keep your hopes up. I mean.... Well, look around you." He sighed. "Things have changed since you arrived. For better or for worse, I honestly don't know."

"Men," Thaddeus called from ahead. "We move out in five minutes."

#

Back on the crumbling streets, Victor rode his gangly steed beside the inquisitors, deeper and deeper into the Leper Quarter. All was silent, save the sounds of hooves against stone and the murmuring chants of a few troopers, until Victor finally spoke up.

"What about Doctor Murdoch?" he called. "Aren't we supposed to be after him too?"

"The suspect will still be alive at day's end, as far as I'm concerned," Thaddeus replied. "I cannot say the same for your friend. Besides, if we are to enter the Inferno, we should access it from where its surges always hit the hardest — the Leper Quarter."

"In layman's terms, we're working on it." Leng threw him a wink.

"Indeed," Thaddeus said. "I am many things, Victor, but honorless is not among them."

"One of your few redeeming qualities," Leng scoffed.

Thaddeus only replied with a gritty growl until he spoke to Victor. "On another note, yesterday you asked me about my tale. If you like, I will tell it."

"Huh?" Victor turned his head, intrigued. "What brought this on?"

"You have told me much of your land and purpose. It is time I told you of mine." Thaddeus caressed that pouch, cradling the set of runic bones. "Leng, if you please."

"Oh, I can't listen too?"

"I'd like to keep the ounce of professionalism we have left."

"I see how it is." Leng sighed, riding off to the rear of the company.

"Contrary to Leng's belief, I was not always a machine-man. I had a childhood like any other," Thaddeus began. "I once lived a friar's life, but also that of a cripple. My limbs were lame, and yet my mind was sharpened like a sword. And as a friar, I was exempt from certain vows of celibacy." He sighed, looking away. "I once had a wife, Victor."

"A wife?" Victor's eyes widened. "You?"

He couldn't really imagine it. Hector Thaddeus, the pious inquisitor of iron flesh and will, feeling such *human* emotion. Despite everything, the conditioning and grafts, there was a man behind all that metal. Someone of humble origins, who was not always this juggernaut.

"Indeed, I was 'quite the looker' before — this." Thaddeus gestured to his respirator. "I remember too the day the Ecclesiarchy declared their holy state. I complied, for this is my nation, but many more did not. For when the uprisings began, she was killed."

Victor's gaze fell upon Leng, who was pretending not to eavesdrop.

"Leng's lost someone too," Victor said. "Seems like the one

181

thing you both have in common." He looked away. "I'm so sorry, Thaddeus. How old were you?"

Thaddeus nodded. "No need to apologize. But I was no older than you, bloodied and broken among the ruins of my home. Lame or not, I swore myself to the Inquisition, and they answered in kind. Eventually, after many a mission, the men of science grafted me with the latest technology." His metallic grip tightened around that pouch. "My wife may be gone to the Empyrean, but I carry her still, cherishing her memory. For it is a sign of wisdom to fetter rage for a greater purpose. I know it is what she would have wanted."

"Goddamn." Victor ran his fingers through his hair. "If you weren't so…honest about it, I'd call you a fascist. But I understand, Thaddeus."

"Fealty, grace, and honor." Thaddeus nodded. "These are the concepts I swear by, and see nothing wrong with them." He looked away. "And yet, even I have my doubts."

"What do you mean?"

"It is relating to the Purgatorio Project," Thaddeus said. "That which was expunged from all records. I have only a shadow of a memory of it. The world was very different before I took that assignment. Contrary to what the Empress would have me think, I can see the shrouds of my misdeeds in the fog. Something happened in Doctor Murdoch's facility, something that changed the world, paving the road to these dark times."

Victor understood Thaddeus's struggle all too well—trying to remember how to be normal. The lost boy was unsure whether to be honored or horrified. Regardless, the inquisitor dared not look Victor in the eye, focusing on the path ahead, as if Thaddeus was distancing his feelings while trying to express them. The hypocrisy of the superman. Victor glanced at Captain Hildegarde, who kept a firm hand over her saber.

"And you can't remember it?" Victor asked.

"No," the inquisitor said. "But I can assume many things. Ever since the project, all the horrors you have seen crept into the city. Before it, the Thirteenth Frequency did not exist, let alone the daemons, or the gruesome serial killings. *If* I was involved in these darkest affairs, then it is my duty to remedy them."

"So that's why you fight," Victor said. "To atone for a sin you can't even remember."

"Yes." Thaddeus turned to Victor as if trying to comfort him. "Not one of us pretends that Holy Gothica is perfect. It is a flawed city, and grievously so. However, it is also a realm with many good people. And by my virtue, I will work within its laws for the greater good. For only a fool knows despair."

"I see."

At that moment Victor felt the weight of Thaddeus's friendship and trust — a sobering sensation, filling his mind with tender anxiety. Then the inquisitor raised his iron fist and the company halted. The pale horses bucked as their riders noticed smoke rising behind a stretch of concrete. Victor could feel his steed's skin wrinkling between his thighs. He shuddered. The fog thickened, but Victor saw a mural of street art along its wall, reading in faded text,

TRAIN GRAVEYARD

Even past the defaced gate Victor smelled a decade's worth of junk and scrap, hearing rasping voices from within. And further inward he saw broken causeways, where ruined locomotives loomed, painted red and yellow. Moreover, calliope music played on old radios, skipping beats here and there, buzzing with static.

"This is our destination," Thaddeus said.

Leng rode to his side. "Not exactly abandoned, is it?"

183

"Curious." Thaddeus readied his electro-staff. "Perhaps we can find information here."

"I doubt it." Leng turned to him, laying a hand over his revolver. "But I guess we have no choice, do we? We have to go in there."

"Indeed." Thaddeus cast light upon another faded sign. "This is also a leper colony. Perhaps they know of our missing person." He turned to the 105th. "Stay put, soldiers."

"Wait. Are we going in alone?" Leng's eyes widened.

Captain Hildegarde said nothing, but Victor could sense ill intent. The stormtroopers all turned to their commander, hands over their rifles, as if contemplating whether or not to open fire. As for why, Victor couldn't even guess. Regardless, Hildegarde shook her head and the soldiers lowered their arms, slowly and silently.

Thaddeus paid them no heed. "This is a delicate matter, and the presence of the stormtroopers would only provoke the lepers. After all, such soldiers are their wardens."

"Lepers are — well, lepers," Leng said. "They're — "

"I do not wish to spill any more blood than need be, Leng." Thaddeus nodded to his deputy and ward. "Both of you, follow me. The way forward is clear."

As the inquisitors dismounted and marched ever onward, Victor stayed put, staring at the vast junkyard ahead. To think, the path to Charles led through that wretched place.

"You should go with your master," the captain said. "Fear not. Though the inquisitor may be foolhardy, we have special orders to — *follow* you, if need be."

"Special orders?" Victor raised an eyebrow. "And what exactly are — ?"

"Victor," Thaddeus called. "Come, your Charles awaits."

CHAPTER EIGHTEEN

Planting his cane against the rubble, Victor stared across the junkyard, his steps shaky down those jagged slopes, feeling along the winding way — until he cut his palm on sharp tin. As Victor and Leng ventured down the winding way, Thaddeus led on with great care, passing by the refuse of industry, under the towers of derelict trains, through the metallic wasteland.

Depressing.

They passed by tar pits and smokestacks, all rust-colored and corroded. The Ecclesiarchy did not bother to survey this sector, leaving its homeless to fester here in the dark. Eventually they came to a village in the valley, a cluster of huts and shacks where lepers brooded about a dying bonfire. Their faces were pallid and poxed, lips bloated. It didn't take long for Victor to realize that the fire was fueled by their dead, like some poor man's crematorium. And looming over the village was a shattered causeway, its old tracks leading to nowhere.

What kind of people are they?

He clutched his cane, its blackthorn chilled by the damp air.

"Listen," Thaddeus said. "There is a reason I gave you that weapon in particular. Bastum is its name. It is the second of its kind, forged and tempered in Azoth pools. As such, it can channel the energy of your soul, tuning your power into a swordsman's skill."

"Meaning," Victor asked, "it only works during the Devil's Hour?"

"Indeed. Such weapons are imperative in our crusades," Thaddeus explained. "In the hands of those touched by the geists, it can cleave the warped flesh of daemons, sending them back to the hells from whence they came."

"I see." Victor twisted the handle, catching a glimpse of its steel blade. "And you're saying I might have to use it."

Thaddeus bowed his head. "Stay close, and do not stray."

Victor's heart sank as he followed the inquisitors, hardly able to breathe. He watched the lepers shoveling filth into wheelbarrows, slamming hammers against anvils, as cowled priests gathered around the pyre, a choir of rasps and whispers.

"Invidia…. Invidia…."

Looming over the shantytown was a wooden chapel, leering over the bonfire, its steeple black against the decay. Every window was nailed shut save for the topmost perch, crowned with a rusty television of dead static — a "window into another world."

"You'll find more cheer in the prisons," Leng muttered under his breath. "We're wasting time here, Thaddeus. Think about contagions! Seriously, this is a bad idea."

"Not until I try something," Thaddeus said. "No sudden movements."

When they came to a rat-catcher's hovel, the inquisitor knocked on the weathered door. It swung open. There stood a miserable old man dressed in rags and scraps, with strands of hair swooping over his brow. He seemed healthier than most of the villagers, leaning on a staff dangling with vermin, a butcher's cleaver by his side.

"Whaddya want?" His breath smelled like a warm morgue. "I ain't done nuthin."

"Your pardon." Thaddeus cleared his throat, raising his iron rosette. "We are agents of Her Holiness's Inquisition. We've come to ask about the late unpleasantries in this area."

"I know what ya are." The rat-catcher spat a wad of black mucus. "It dun take a fancy boy from up there to know. Who else would come to the Train Graveyard?" He turned to the burning pyre. "I said, I ain't done nuthin!" He bared his filed teeth and clenched his fists, skin rotting and motley. "Get out my face, before I rip yours off!"

"Yeah, he's lost it," Leng whispered to Victor, hand over his holster. "Too far gone to be of any help." He cleared his throat. "We appreciate your understanding, ser."

When they turned around Victor's nausea festered staring at the pole rising from the bonfire, where the corpses of several troopers loomed, impaled to the stake. And as one of the chanting monks turned his head, Victor saw that the priest wore a doll mask.

"Look out!" Leng's voice cracked.

Victor spun around and saw a crazed look in the rat-catcher's eyes as he lifted the cleaver above his head, a mad butcher. Gunshots echoed in the distance, followed by bloodcurdling cries. Victor lunged away as Thaddeus sliced the leper's chest open in a haze of gore.

Oh shit!

Thaddeus turned around, eyes wide with terror and wrath. Another leper jerked its head and raised a finger, shouting in an urban dialect Victor couldn't understand. The inquisitors' eyes narrowed upon the torches and pitchforks, upon true heretics.

W-what…? Are they even still human?

The priests led a shambling mob into the light. They were a hideous lot, some wearing masks and others capirotes, but all draped with soiled robes and talismans of teeth and twigs. In bandaged hands they clutched maces and sabers, laden with marks of a great evil.

"Men of the Imperium." Their leader spoke in a wet rasp, clutching a jointed staff of uncured bone. "We will take your hides, hang them from our crossings and lattices, and sing songs of your dying screams." His veins bulged. "Bring me their teeth!"

They swarmed forth, more like roaches than men. As one raised its blade, Thaddeus dodged and gutted the leper, spilling his cancerous entrails onto the ground. While Victor took cover behind a hut, the inquisitors stood back to back. Leng's every bullet hit its mark, but whether by divine will or marksmanship, none could say. Thaddeus, blade coated in blood, stood his ground, and as time dragged on, his staff's light faded, barely keeping the mob at bay.

With a hollow click, Leng realized he was almost out of bullets.

Then the world turned gray and vivid. Victor cradled his forehead, feeling the whispers of the Cacophony spilling from the church's antennae, a surge creeping into reality.

The Thirteenth Frequency?

That random power spared Victor and the inquisitors, and a majority of the lepers, as if chosen by the Cacophony. Others were not so lucky, transfigured into faceless mannequins, petrified by the will of daemons, oblivious to such malevolence until the hour's end.

The battle was not yet over.

Two lepers lunged, swinging at Victor's head. There was a newfound madness in their eyes, a yellowed evil not of this world. But Victor was nimble, able to dodge their blows, until he drew his sword from that shillelagh for the first time in combat. In his hands Bastum echoed with the Music of the Spheres, glowing with cobalt light, filling Victor with valor. Readying his blade, he stabbed one in the gut and sliced up, the wound splashing a familiar black bile. As that cultist collapsed, another one swung and cut Victor's bicep.

Fuck!

He cried out as blood splattered the cobblestones. A boot slammed against his chest, sending Victor flat on his back. As he wheezed, a leper pulled out a pair of pliers. He yanked Victor's head back, lowering the tongs towards his teeth, cackling like a hyena. Heart pounding, Victor reached for his blade until he felt the hilt in his grasp.

As Victor slashed up, he felt his willpower manifest to its blade, smoldering with blue flame. With strength he did not know he possessed, he cleaved the leper's head clean off. But to his horror the peasant shambled back, and from its neck sprung tentacles of black ooze — the limbs of a daemon. Victor staggered away, but retained what was left of his courage. He impaled the host with a squelching thrust, and it collapsed to its knees.

There came an eardrum-shattering shriek. Victor was overwhelmed with a seizure of bad thought. Static consumed his mind whole, numbing all rational thought with panic. Voices filled the gaps in his gray matter, jammed into the few cubic centimeters inside his skull.

W-what kind of surge is this?

Bastum's light dulled to chrome then, but Victor felt his own power throbbing in the sword yet, waiting to be awakened once more. Driving past his agony, Victor's senses slowly returned. Thaddeus hoisted him up, and they beheld the lifeless limbo of the city. No color remained, as if all the world had been swallowed by eternal darkness.

#

Victor's arm was wrought with stabbing pain. Thaddeus drew a salve pouch and rubbed a generous helping on Victor's wound. It burned like acid, but the bleeding stopped soon enough.

Victor's face grew pale, remembering the Dollmaker's latest threat.

After the Devil's Hour, there might not be a friend to find.

"We cannot linger," Thaddeus said. "Let us be off."

Leng looked over his shoulder. "Shouldn't we wait for the 105th?"

Victor shuddered, the agony still fresh in his mind. "Those lepers were possessed, weren't they? But you don't think they're behind all this, do you?"

"They were a cult. I suspect one founded on spite and despair." Thaddeus turned to one of the petrified statues. "But are they behind the murders? This I doubt. Horrible as they are, all registered lepers are confined to the ghettos. And these people strike me as lacking the skill to direct the surges. But let me contact our company." He drew his codec, only to stare at a blank screen. "Dammit, I always forget that the Vox is useless during these events."

Leng grew pale. "Don't tell me we're on our own."

"I am afraid so." Thaddeus turned towards the broken causeway, a fleeting shadow against the thickening fog. "And I have a strong feeling this attack was planned."

Leng's eyes widened. "Wait—we were expected?"

"Indeed," Thaddeus said. "But I wonder, since when do such rabbles plan their attacks?"

As the inquisitors discussed their next course of action,

Victor turned to the tin church in the village square. It had been salvaged from mere scrap, and yet Victor felt there was more to it than that. Just what lay inside its nave? Perhaps something worth searching?

There was a guttural wheeze from under his nose.

"Why don't you ask?" Leng turned to a wounded leper. "We got a live one."

A young leper lay down, dazed, trying to reach for his mace, fingers trembling. Thaddeus marched forward and kicked the weapon aside, pointing his sword at the vagabond's throat.

"Unless you lack the conviction, kill me." The cultist gritted his teeth, as if trying to mask his terror. "I have nothing left to fear."

"Bold words." Thaddeus dug his blade into the leper's skin. "Do not mistake me for some Puritan fool. Know that I too suffered loss and despair. However, I swore myself to order, and did not wallow in pity. Your ilk are a scourge. The weak who fell to temptation."

"What do you know of pain?" The leper retorted, black bile oozing like tears. "It is your false god who remained silent in my darkest hour, condemning me to this self-sustaining death camp." He spat at Thaddeus's feet. "Your guilty all rot in one prison of neglect. No, do not talk to me of loss, Inquisitor. You know nothing of it."

"The Cacophony clouds your vision," Thaddeus replied, "and like the leprosy, I cannot cure it. But our god is *not* silent." He withdrew the runic bones of his wife. "All are equal in His eyes. I shall call upon Him to decide your fate. You will go free, or die here and now."

The leper raised a quivering hand. "Wait. If I tell you why I am here, may I go?"

Thaddeus said nothing.

191

"Our priests told us to make preparations for intruders." The leper's eyes fell upon the church, lips curling into a mad smile. "They were leading us in prayer to our *new* god. One who will not abandon us. The true savior who avenges the fallen." He stared at Victor. "Such is our road to salvation. To be absolved through the depths of Hell."

Hell?

"You feel it as well, don't you?" The leper licked his lips. "The hallowed power behind the screens. In that world within our world, we see the true nature of ourselves, do we not? The good, the bad, and the worst. All born of sin. You call them daemons."

"You're working for the Dollmaker," Victor snapped, "aren't you?"

"Dollmaker?" The leper hissed. "No, don't be a fool. Our faith is not one of murdering whores. Our lord's plan is far more — *interesting* than that. Tonight, our priests felt a power in that innermost world. An omen of envy. And so, we honored that spirit." He turned to Thaddeus. "I have told you everything. May I go? What good is it to kill me?"

"What is your name, heretic?" Thaddeus asked. "Your given name?"

"I can't remember." The leper looked away. "It's been so long since I've—"

"And pity will not save you." Thaddeus tossed the bones in the air, and when they landed the leper shed a black tear. "Your false brothers will carry on without you. And yet, I know your soul will be absolved at the Pearly Gates." He stared the cultist dead in the eye, raising his sword as an executioner. "I shall regret nothing, and yet...."

The leper shut his eyes, shaking, as if accepting his fate.

"I will show you mercy." Thaddeus lowered the blade,

turning his back. "A rarity indeed. But if we cross paths ever again," he hissed, "I will not go so gentle."

"Wait," Leng objected. "You can't just let him go!"

"If I recall," Thaddeus barely kept his composure, "you were assigned to prevent me from carrying out summary executions. Do you dare defy that charge, *Ser* Walter Leng?"

"B-but...."

Thaddeus shot him a piercing glare, sharp enough to cut Leng's words short and thin. "Go, you wretch." He turned to the leper. "Now."

With that the leper staggered up, his lips quivering, as if about to thank the inquisitor, but he dared not speak. Instead, he limped away, as fast as he could, down the junkyard road.

"Do you understand," Thaddeus asked Victor, "why I showed him mercy?"

"I understand why. But...." He shoved his hands into his pockets. "When you first met me in the prisons, and used those bones. Would you have killed me, if they demanded it?"

Thaddeus's eyes insinuated many things, but he did not speak, nor would he ever answer that question. For to Victor, some things were best left unknown, even between brothers in arms.

However, when the inquisitors were about to leave, Victor heard whispers in the stagnant air. Just then, the television atop the "church" flashed on. An image took form, rippling beyond and behind the static. Victor saw the silhouette of Charles in the aether, warped by fog, stretching out a hand. Then a vast shadow emerged, dragging his friend into the void.

"Victor," Thaddeus called, "don't do anything foolish."

Panic welled in Victor's chest—panic masking valor. "You said the TVs were portals to the Inferno," he said. "Is it a one-way door?"

"Oh, shut up, Victor." Leng gawked. "You don't mean—"

"It's simple. When this surge ends, Charles dies." Victor turned to a ladder up the shingles. "We have to do this if we want to save him. There's no way around it."

He began to climb, knees shaking with doubt, forcing himself up. As Victor peered into the television, he saw the silhouette of an impossible tower. He feared the worst, but no matter how long he stared, Victor couldn't muster the courage to cross over.

Thaddeus joined him. "Are you sure about this? There is no shame in turning back."

"I'm sure," he mustered. "I didn't come this far to weasel my way out."

"I see." Thaddeus looked away. "Your pardon. What is your plan after finding your missing friends? You seem to be flying blind, Victor. This does not bode well. And while I encourage you to stay with us, prophecies cannot be forced. You wish to leave, do you not?"

"Thaddeus—"

"I understand full well," his mentor continued. "We inquisitors are conditioned to accept the horrors of the fate. But some things can scar even the most jaded of souls." His hand fell upon the bone-pouch. "You are stronger than you think, Victor."

Victor looked away. "You hardly know me."

"But I know what drives you," Thaddeus said. "The will to do good, even in the face of impossible darkness. To protect and love, to *create*, until all worldly pleasures are but—dust in the wind." He nodded. "And one day, you will understand that such love is the cornerstone of all godliness, even in this rotting world of mine."

"And that's what started this for you? *Love?*"

"Yes." Thaddeus rubbed his iron fingers against the bag of bones. "He who acknowledges compassion, and acts upon it, is closer to truth and faith than any knight templar. Cherish your loved ones, Victor. I shall say no more on the matter."

Time was running out. Victor knew, deep down, that he could only hide for so long. A choice would have to be made. He drew a shuddering breath and shoved a hand into the screen, swallowed by numbness. At first Victor was shocked, but accepted this phenomenon as fact.

"The power to enter the screens," Thaddeus said. "You possess it as well?"

Leng's eyes widened. "Yeah, I thought only the Dollmaker could do that."

Driven by determination alone, Victor dove headfirst into the unknown, swept by an overwhelming tide of darkness—into the otherworld which underpinned Holy Gothica. A realm born of nightmares and wicked distortion.

The fogbound depths of Hell.

CHAPTER NINETEEN

Adrift in mental oblivion, cobalt lights danced in Victor's skull. Sure enough, the balconies and velvet curtains of the Opera House materialized out of the fog. And as he felt the carpet under his boots, Victor turned to the oaken stage where the Impresario sat and leered.

"Your powers are growing," he said, lifting his long nose. "Power enough to perhaps save your dear friend. Even so, the road to maturity must be pursued with vim and vigor."

Victor ran his fingers through his hair. "Well, like I said, I'm doing this for my friends." He looked away. "That being said, my choices are running out fast."

The Impresario's smile did not fade. "Indeed. For a moment, I was unsure if you would survive that encounter in the Leper Quarter. But you triumphed, and dove into the realm of true madness. A most admirable decision, even if driven by selfish intent."

Victor stared at the carpet. "Just tell me Charles is alive."

"The fog is growing quite thick, Victor," the Impresario said. "Thick enough to waylay even the most cautious of travelers. You must brave it in order to find the truth. However, you still do not believe in the prophecy. You still deny your role in this world."

"Yeah, you're right," Victor retorted. "I don't think I'm the Far Messiah. I never was one for prayer, and I don't want to be worshipped. I have enough narcissistic tendencies as it is, and I'm not about to let my ego get the better of me. Not again. I've *been* down that road."

The Impresario nodded. "I see. That conviction will be tested soon enough."

"Understood." A waking haze consumed Victor's mind. "I think I'll live...."

#

"Victor," a familiar voice called. "Victor!"

He awoke, greeted by cold metal against his flesh. Groping the railing, Victor slowly stood and regained his wits, mind buzzing with static and fear. Thaddeus scanned the smog bound horizon, while Leng leaned against an iron support. Every step was a hollow clunk over the abyss, and Victor shivered at the otherworldly atmosphere.

"Ah." Thaddeus turned around. "I see you've come through."

Leng rolled his eyes. "If I had a copper for every time you passed out...."

Victor cradled his skull. This world was different than the city of cathedrals. It was a framework suspended over a sea of damned souls, reeking of burnt plastic and brimstone. Victor squinted against the floodlights, sweating under their raw heart. Beyond the wires, he saw a sky of spiraling swirls—a dead channel of hypnosis.

"Damn," Leng said. "I can't see a thing with all this smog."

"We need more light," Thaddeus chimed in, activating what power remained in his electro-staff, shimmering like a dying star in the void. "A slight improvement."

"Hardly," Leng coughed. "This place is oppressive."

Victor stared in terrible awe. "Where *are* we?"

No one replied, for no one rightly knew. However, a fleeting sense of determination filled Victor's pounding heart, and the inquisitors carried on until they saw something in the distance.

What is that…?

It was a never-ending spire out of an expressionist film. Its depths were far and bottomless, and yet its turrets spiraled ever upward, into the endless miasma above. Stained glass windows depicted torture and devilry, twisting along its parapets, all in a labyrinthine haze of wings and wards — an Escheresque bastion of whimsy and horror.

"The Inferno." Thaddeus blessed his brow. "The underworld of our souls and shadows, and the birthplace of our innermost daemons."

Victor gawked. "You mean, this is Hell? Literally?"

"It is chaos primordial, yes," Thaddeus replied. "If our city is of the mortal realm, this is a reflection of the minds of men, and how warped they are." He shuddered. "A palace of sin."

"Yeah," Leng said. "I suppose if someone gets stuck here, it might reflect their thoughts first and foremost. A self-tailored nightmare. All those hookers probably died here too."

"Then," Victor began to sweat, "this place was born of Charles's 'sin'?"

Indeed, it was not the generic hellscape he had envisioned. It was far more personal than that. As the fog lifted, the tower revealed its current form. Its turrets were crowned with big tops and Ferris wheels, beastly cages hanging from gibbets, every battlement a house of mirrors, as railroad tracks snaked around the "attractions."

And the archway read in crimson font,

CIRQUE DU CHARLEMAGNE

Time had no meaning here. Some minutes felt like hours, and some hours were as minutes. Here, all the world was a stage.

Victor squinted past the stinging smog. Most of these paths were nigh identical, until the abstract began to materialize into its own "reality."

"Is Charles really in there?" Victor asked himself. "Is he even alive?"

"I know not," Thaddeus replied. "We must search this hell if we are to find him."

"Heh," Leng said. "Doesn't it look like a gypsy circus?"

"Do you allow circuses in your city?" Victor asked.

"Well, yeah," Leng replied. "How else are we supposed to celebrate 'the Grand Conductor's will'? By sitting in a confessional and whipping ourselves? Good for the flagellants, sure. Not so much for the everyman." He sighed. "You have a lot to learn, kid."

"Wait." Victor paused. "So if the city has its circuses, and Charles worked in a circus—in my world, I mean—is there a correlation somehow?"

"Perhaps so," Thaddeus said. "It may explain that herbal reek as well. This could be the world through your friend's eyes."

Truth be told, Victor did smell the lingering scent of "hash 'n pot," as Charles would put it.

Just in front of the fairgrounds proper lay a train station, its clock tower leering, ticking along to a thirteenth hour. Victor clutched his shillelagh, creeping up those iron steps.

Then, an eerie whistle pierced the smog.

Victor turned his head and saw it. The Dreadtrain rolled across a track of charred bones, suspended over the boiling sea of blood. The first thing he noticed was something painted on the engine—Charles's face, rosy-cheeked and exaggerated, like the uncanny facade of a carnival. And its nose glowed with a scarlet light, slowing and screeching ever into vision.

"Come one, come all," said a bombastic voice, "to the Cirque du Charlemagne! Come see the one-man troupe with a thousand faces. Can you guess which is the true self? Can you peer through the masks and pierce the darkness within? Test your skill and wits, but be warned." It uttered a cruel chuckle. "This challenge is not for the faint of heart!"

Victor's eyes widened with horror, beginning to understand this place.

The Dreadtrain was laden with battlements and buttresses of obsidian, cars shaped as naves, ducts belching ash and smoke through the gargoyles' mouths. Worse yet was its decor and imagery—peace signs and pot leaves, tie-dyes of reds and blacks, its smokestacks polluting all with the reek of cannabis and fresh blood. It came to a creaking halt, doors opening wide.

"So," Leng said, "that's the dungeon?"

"None other." Thaddeus clutched his electro-staff. "This is the First Circle, tailored to Charles's doubts and fears. Be on guard and tread lightly, lest such an abyss reap our souls."

As Victor stepped forward, something fell from his pocket. He knelt and picked up the toy rabbit. Feeling its cotton, Victor heard an aria of his own composition, recalling the Opera House and the power of geist. Sure enough, the miasma of the Inferno blurred as a familiar voice echoed in his mind's ear.

"Thus," the Impresario said, "it finally begins. Remember your power, and wield it well. For the darkness that we spoke of encroaches upon your dearest friend. And it will strike harder than ever." He chuckled. "Only you can save him."

I'm either a hero or an idiot.

And so, Victor tucked the rabbit in his pocket, boarding into blackness.

#

The air was thick and moist, flies buzzing throughout the passenger car. And when the blacklights flickered on, Victor and the inquisitors beheld a casino draped over a chapel—red and black, and slimy green. Mustard-colored tarps were draped over lines of pews, the gothic decor highlighted by tightropes and striped rings, floral patterns, and peace signs—relics of 1969.

They were memories of a dear friend, defiled by the darkness of infinity.

Like if Tim Burton threw up in Woodstock.

He heard strange music—a strumming guitar of classic rock, accompanied by sinister synth and tambourine chimes, the marching drums of Jefferson Airplane, and the humming choir of the Lemon Pipers. Victor kept his wits about him, but these songs were corrupted. Listening to their evil melodies, he knew that something vile was at work.

"You hear it as well." Thaddeus guided him along. "Don't you?"

"It's the Cacophony, isn't it?"

Thaddeus nodded. "Indeed. We must be—"

Victor heard the doors slam behind them, and a wave of cold sweat flooded his body. The car quivered as he heard the revolutions of its wheels.

"Shit!" Leng pushed and pulled at the door. "Open! Open, dammit!"

"It is no use," Thaddeus hissed, as if trying to mask failing composure. "Knowing the canon, we must head to the heart of Hell, and exorcise whatever daemon lurks within." He turned to Victor. "No doubt the same thing is holding your friend hostage."

The Dreadtrain rolled ever onward on the rickety tracks, like a rollercoaster racing to certain destruction. Victor gazed out the windows and saw the funhouses and Ferris wheels of that twisted carnival. Then he heard someone in the distance, someone all too familiar—a voice carried by the wind, screaming, contorted by fog and static.

"Shut! Up! Get out of my head, you sick bastard!"

Victor bolted, almost tripping over a splintered floorboard. "Charles? Is that you?!"

There was no response, only a monstrous laugh fading towards the farthest engine.

"Goddammit," he hissed. "Hang in there, dude."

Though Victor's stomach sank, he knew he couldn't dwell on this. If Charles was here, then he would find him. Victor shuddered, swaying as the train shook, feeling his way along the rusty railing. At the car's end he pressed open the next door, into the Hall of Mirrors, each reflection distorted by twisting images of the self.

"Victor!" Thaddeus's words bounced off his ears. "Be careful. Do not stray!"

Victor kept a hand on Bastum, his sacred blade, bracing himself for the worst. He kept his eyes glued to the floor, not daring to look into the mirrors. As he dashed down the curving corridors, a sharp chord bounced off the walls. Doll masks rippled from the cracks, surrounded by black bile, until they oozed and splashed down, only to rise as motley jesters.

Victor staggered back, eyes wide.

Lips painted with evil smiles, their fingers ended in bloodletting claws, all frilled collars and pointed shoes. Writhing, they spun in a waltz, faster and faster, laughing mad all the while. They mimicked Charles's voice with droning lyrics, in tune to the Rolling Stones.

"Never got to tell Victor how I really felt...."

Though Victor readied his sword cane, those words had an insidious power to them, draining all strength and hope. He tried to move, but was petrified by dread and depression—bombarded by memories of the times he and Charles had spent together.

The time I walked him home after a night of drinking. We ended up playing old-school Mario Kart until the sun rose, surrounded by dime bags and porno mags. The time he threw a house party. Everyone who showed up was either a Vietnam veteran or an anarchist who'd seen the Berkeley riots. The time he tried to hook me up with a blind date with a single mom. We ended up just relaxing at the bar when she never showed up.

"Away with you, lying ones!" Thaddeus called, lifting his electro-staff, its light radiating from mirror to mirror, a beacon of hope against the slathering daemons, dazzling them. "Go back to the nothingness which spawned you!"

Victor snapped back to the present, regaining his balance. As the daemons closed in, he felt a roar welling in his throat. "Dante," he screamed, feeling the toy rabbit burn in his grip, taking form once more. "Come forth!"

With a buzz of firing neurons, Victor's summon warped into existence again—a crimson-cowled figure, born of nostalgia, ears long and drooping. Like a Venetian knight, its mask was adorned with musical symbols, staring on with a single eye. Floating above and behind Victor, it clutched that lunar halberd, prepared for battle.

The clowns bowed and pranced, soaring with cruel vigor.

Dante dove forward as music and might flowed through Victor. And when its halberd dug deep into a doll mask, the geist slashed outward and the clown burst into bile and smoke.

Victor smiled, feeling the vibrations of Dante's blow as an extension of his will.

Another wall of mirrors shattered, releasing dust and living shadows.

And so, Dante swung again, slicing its blade into a "burning man." Its mask splintered, and the geist charged with strength Victor didn't know it had, as if possessed by his lucid imagination. One after another the daemons fell to Victor's guardian, until he spun around and saw a sideshow freak rush at him, with hollow eyes and needle teeth. Doubling back, he almost tripped as the daemon outstretched its razored claws.

"Away with you, sin spawn!" Thaddeus roared.

With a stab and slice the inquisitor cut the daemon down, just as Victor felt its claws dig into his arm before dissolving into black mist. And then, there was only silence.

"Those daemons," Thaddeus murmured. "They were no doubt tailored to Charles's psyche. No longer are they abstract embodiments of mankind's sins. They are something far more personal and dangerous now. Aware of our presence."

Many thoughts raced through Victor's mind as he staggered on.

Dwelling on that won't save him. Those times were awesome, sure, but we have many more to share. There has to be. Charles, I will find you....

"Dammit." Victor shuddered to think of him, trapped among his own thoughts and fears. "We have to keep going." He pointed to the door ahead. "Seems like we're almost halfway."

Leng chuckled, lagging behind, hands in his pockets.

Victor scowled. "What's so funny?"

"Oh, nothing." Leng looked away. "I just remembered the pussyfooting kid from a few days ago. I wonder what ever happened to him?" He looked Victor in the eye. "You're changing, and I'm kinda proud of you. It's good that you care about something this much. Enough to let your balls drop." He turned to a mirror. "Hell, even I don't have that—"

"We can exchange praise later," Thaddeus hissed. "Must I always remind you to stay on track, Leng?" The inquisitor took a few steps forward, pausing before his ward. "That's not to say he isn't right. Lead the way, Victor."

#

Driven by sheer determination, Victor stormed ahead, door after door, feeling the Music of the Spheres coursing from the tarot cards, casting light upon mental voids like stars of fleeting hope.

Then, he halted before the final car of the Dreadtrain.

Victor was overcome with a sense of responsibility for all that had happened to his friends. His head swam in a sea of self-loathing. As for Thaddeus and Leng, this was not their fight; they had already done so much for him. This was something Victor had to do alone.

"Wait here," Victor mustered, drawing his sacred blade. "I'll go in alone."

"What?" Leng stopped dead in his tracks. "Are you *insane*?"

"Seriously. This last part doesn't concern you two." Victor forced a trembling smile. "Besides, you and Thaddeus were after the Dollmaker before all this. If anything, I derailed your mission. But I just want to say, thanks for everything." He felt the plushness of the rabbit in his pocket. "In the end, this is my responsibility."

Thaddeus pulled him back. "You cannot do this."

"Yeah, we have no idea what's in there," Leng said. "Only that it's bad. *Really* bad. Aren't you afraid? You heard that cultist. Charles could be dead for all we know, and—"

"There is no courage without fear." Victor turned to

Thaddeus. "Am I wrong?"

Thaddeus's grip slowly loosened. "Bless your foolish hope," he sighed. "I have no right to stop you, Victor. But if something should happen, I do not know what I shall do. I think of you as something of a — friend." And for the first time, Victor heard Thaddeus utter a laugh, however bitter. "Yes. A *friend*. How strange it feels to say that."

"Shit," Leng scoffed. "Never expected you two to get all buddy-buddy when my back was turned." He bit his lip. "Just be careful in there, okay?"

Victor nodded, savoring what light remained.

Dark thoughts raced through his mind, swallowed by a sea of anxiety. The doorway leered like a mocking grimace and he shuddered. Could he even do this? What lurked behind that door? Would Dante be enough this time? Or, was it too late?

No, it doesn't matter. I have to save Charles. He's all I have left.

Victor turned one last time to Thaddeus and Leng, and saw tender looks in their eyes. He took a deep breath and plunged into the darkness, as that iron door locked itself behind him.

Too late to turn back.

CHAPTER TWENTY

Victor's knees quivered as he beheld the nave of black comedy, its walls laced with massive televisions. Something trickled on his brow. He looked up, eyes drawn by slabs of flesh hanging from meat hooks, swaying like reeking chandeliers. Victor's stomach bubbled and churned as his eyes narrowed upon the boiler—a throbbing womb of cables and ducts, powering those convex screens. As smog leaked into the great chamber, Victor heard heavy breathing from above.

Is that…?

His eyes lifted to see Charles suspended on a saltire of iron, bonds tight on his gangly arms and legs. That cross was surrounded by whirligig saws and torturous needles, no doubt designed to extract the vitae from the prisoner.

When Victor called and stuttered, his friend's eyes rolled open.

"Victor?" Charles smiled with blistered lips. "Dude, you really there?"

"Y-yeah, it's me." He masked tears welling behind his eyes, voice wavering. Seeing him was all too surreal. After all this time—after all they'd been through. "You look *horrible*. Don't

207

worry, I'll get you out of here. Just give me a second."

Victor looked about for a lever or a pulley. Something. Anything.

"Will do," Charles scoffed, trying to keep his cool. "So, how've you been?"

"Oh, you know," Victor said. "Accosted by the Inquisition, press-ganged into prophecy, summoning geists out of my skull. The usual."

"Dude…." Charles raised an eyebrow. "The fuck have you been smoking, and can I have some?" As Victor tried to figure out an escape, he and Charles caught up on their misadventures in this wretched world. "So, you're basically Jesus with Asperger's now?"

"Debatably," Victor replied. "I mean, it makes sense. Maybe I indirectly *made* this world. But still, it doesn't explain why this hell exists. I mean, it's clearly mirroring *your* memories and whatnot." He lowered his head. "Remember that carnival?"

"How could I not?" Charles said, struggling against the metal bonds with what strength he had left. The rusty cross creaked and swayed. "And yeah, this place has my name written all over it. It even smells like weed." He laughed somberly. "Beatrice would have a field day with this."

"How is she? Alive, I hope."

"Better than me, but that's not saying much." Charles looked away. "Punk rock chick joins rebellion. Nothing's really changed since I was a kid."

Victor smiled. "I'm just glad she's out there."

"She's actually the one who told me about you being alive." Charles jerked his head, trying to get his silver bangs out of his eyes. "I actually tried looking for you, just before everything went down. I wanted to save you. Looks like it turned out the other way around."

Victor's eyes widened. "That's stupid of you."

"Hey, you'd do the same for me." A spliff fell from behind Charles's ear; he frowned. "Dammit. Could you get that for me? Probably not the best time to get high, though."

"You damn pothead," Victor chuckled, and picked up the joint. He tugged at a few chains and pulled a final lever. The cross descended with a rickety *clunk*, and the iron cuffs released. Charles fell onto his knees but stood up, cracking his back.

"How do you fit into all this?" Victor asked. "Do you have any—?

"Any epic quests or daemon hunting? Not a whole lot." Charles took the spliff back with shaky hands. "Well, I did hear a voice telling me to 'awaken,' or something."

"Hang on," Victor mustered. "Was it some kind of archaic voice? Because that's how I was able to summon my geist. Who knows, you might have some power, too."

"Nah." Charles smiled sadly. "I'm probably second fiddle in these cosmic schemes. Can't say I'm that surprised, but...." He stared out a window upon the twisting towers of the Inferno. "Dude, do you ever have that feeling? That your own brain is out to get you?"

"I think we both know that feeling," Victor replied. "What brought this on?"

"Deep down, I'm filled with regret." Charles shuddered. "All my life I've been running from myself. Just like this train. Trapped in one direction. Riding away from the truth. And now, I don't even have that. I've taken on so many gigs over the years—bartender, paraeducator—chicken suit guy. They're all parts of me, but not actually me."

"What do you mean? You're Charles."

"And I have a face I put on for you too."

The lights flickered and dimmed, and Charles's shadow

extended across the engine, like a blight upon this reality. As the wheels below shrieked and moaned like tortured beasts, Victor felt something else, something that made his friend wince in pure terror.

Then the "music" returned—heartbeats pounding along to Metallica.

"Well, well." The shadow moved on its own, taking the form of the "other" Charles—the daemon with the tea shades, its voice a distorted echo. "How does it feel, Victor? To know your self-righteous crusade drove away your friends? Your reality? It's like a bad trip on DMT."

The hell? Two of Charles?

"Oh God," Charles whimpered. "No, no. Not again." Before he could say anything else, a storm of fog burst from the ducts and pipes, obscuring Charles and his doppelganger in a mist bound haze. "Victor," he screamed. "H-help!"

Victor lunged forward. The mist churned like a whirlpool of despair, it's burning gales keeping him from getting any closer. "Charles!" Panic welled his throat. "*Charles!*"

"And since the heroic lead got taken…." The voice boomed over Charles's terrified screams. "I'll gladly play the villain. More fun, anyway. How does that feel?"

Strings sang against the throbbing bass—Victor stood his ground. "I call bullshit!" he snapped. "I know you're in there somewhere. Please! You're my *best* friend."

"Shut up! Don't you get it? There's nothing for me here," the voice snapped. "You know nothing about me, Victor. You may pretend you do, but you don't know me at all. We drink. We talk. But what have we actually done together? Nothing!"

Those words cut and impaled their friendship. Victor stepped back and began to question the entire reason he'd journeyed so far. But as the tears flowed, he felt the Cacophony brewing like a storm over the roiling sea, realizing what was really happening.

The daemons – they're the darkness in our hearts. This daemon – a powerful one at that. Is it channeling from the depths of Charles's mind? Corrupting it?

"No!" Victor outstretched a hand. The tarot cards rushed to his side, wreathed in cobalt flame, their righteous power buzzing throughout his mind. "Let him go! I'm not going to let you end it. Not like this. Even if it means rebuking the living shit out of you."

The Cacophony intensified, its daemons growling and squealing, unseen.

"You thought I was so funny, didn't you? Yeah, I was your *clown*." It gave a throbbing chuckle, and the gas lamps turned black, causing evil images to glow in the unlight. Cards and dice were all defaced by the skeletal and macabre, serrated with bloody spikes and blades. Victor stumbled as the floor lifted as a neon roulette wheel. "That'll be the day. I will kill you, or you will kill me. It makes no difference."

"I never thought I'd say this." Victor stared on, unblinking, and by defiant will alone mustered, "But f-fuck you, man! Come out of the fog and fight me."

"Alright-a. I have nothing to hide!" The voice rose to a laughing cry, warped beyond recognition. There was an explosion of darkness from the purple haze, sending Charles skidding across the raised arena. "Everything your friend kept from you, I embody. Every doubt, every fear, every inkling of envy. I am the failure you never knew!"

"Charles!" Victor screamed, rushing to his friend's side. "Are you okay?"

"I'm sorry. So—so sorry." Charles tried to stand, only to slump onto his bleeding knees, head in his hands, shaking and sobbing. "P-please don't listen to it. Please."

Victor turned to the bloated shadow looming and leering over them. "What *is* this?"

"Lies," he tried to speak. "Just lies...." Charles staggered up, brushing away his tears and the splinters on his shins. "You're a monster! You can't be *me*, you son of a bitch!"

A moment of fleeting silence passed.

"Yeah, that's right," the voice said. "I'm not *you*. Not anymore. I am the Daemon of Envy. The daemon that rules the crazy train and this circus of insanity!"

The Cacophony returned, rising into a crescendo of madness. The "medley" of metal broke into a shredding guitar, warped by discord, blasting into Victor's flinching ears.

A massive pair of marionette hands lunged from the clouds, dancing on strings, flashing peace signs before forming fists, slamming into the columns like wooden wrecking balls. Victor narrowly dodged them, feeling them soar past his skull.

Jesus!

With that the haze lifted, and they beheld that darkest puppeteer—a giant ventriloquist's dummy, carved like a stage magician, its "face" stretched by an impossible mouth, filled with row upon row of crooked fangs, eyes sinking into the side of its skull. Reminiscent of a clown's corpse, it slobbered and oozed black bile. With a chimney of a top hat, its body was a slot machine of copper and sinew, napalm fueling its gears and lathes, scorching its pallid flesh. For this was the medium between Charles's mind and Hell itself.

"Oh my God," he gawked.

"Yeah! You're better off dead." The Ringmaster's voice was that of an old-time villain over a broken radio. "Come on, you thought it over before—*many* times in the city. Checking the dosage on that pill bottle. Fiddling with the trigger." It raised a puppeted palm, as if to swat Charles like a gnat. Out of sheer reflex, Victor tackled him aside, feeling a shockwave upon the hand's landing. "But it's not really 'suicide' if I do it, right?"

Victor knew what to do.

"Motherfucker," Charles wheezed. "This can't be happening. It can't—"

"Dante!" Victor called. The tarot cards soared and spiraled about as he tossed the toy rabbit in the air, engulfed in cobalt flames once more. "Let's end this."

With a buzz of forceful will, Victor felt his geist warp into existence again, masked with music and nobleness, ears long and drooping. A symphony of neurons sang against the evil of Charles's soul—strings, brass, and woodwinds, all in allegro and forte. For Dante soared above and behind Victor, clutching its lunar halberd, its marble eye burning with resolve.

"Don't worry, dude." Victor tried to smile, drawing his sword. "I got your back."

#

The Ringmaster lashed out with its fists, but Victor leapt to the side, tumbling with dexterous skill. And by his will Dante glided about, slicing, parrying each blow that came too close, staring on with a single, stoic eye. Victor let the Music of the Spheres flow through him. Even as those hands swept and soared, he felt a holy rhythm reverberating in his soul, carrying him and the geist against the darkness of Charles's heart.

"No matter what you do, nothing will change," the Ringmaster chuckled, lowering its wooden hands. "You will always be second-rate. And I refuse to be shackled to you anymore." It spun the elevated arena as Victor and Charles collapsed atop each other in a daze. "I'm tired of being the laughing stock. The ass-end of every joke."

"God-fucking-dammit!" Charles gritted his teeth, drawing

his revolver, only to hear a series of empty clicks. "Stop it! You're nothing like me—"

"You'll have to do a lot better than that," the Ringmaster hissed. "What? Do you think your faux friendship will save you?" A palm descended towards them, like a ton of steel. They rolled to the left as it landed with a quaking thud. Charles and Victor staggered up, staring at the daemon where its face should have been. "This is our dream now. And we're never waking up!" It hissed like a coiled serpent; the slot machines spun and spun, faster and faster, until they hit all doll masks and crossbones. "And the best part is, you know it's the truth."

"Shut! Up!" Charles screamed, tears streaming down his face.

The Ringmaster let loose an ear-splitting shriek, calling upon the darkness of discord, and lesser daemons oozed from cracks in the neon panels. Charles stifled a cry of terror. They were miserable things of painted masks and bells and caps—jesters of a hollow heart.

"There's too many!" Charles stepped back. "We gotta blow this joint, dude."

"Like *hell* we are." Victor outstretched a trembling hand. "Slay them, Dante!"

Thus the geist descended upon the imps and fools, severing a number of them with a mighty cleave, like a knife through rancid butter.

Meanwhile, Victor dodged a daemon swinging its scissor-blade and sliced open its belly, black blood sputtering as it dissolved. The others jittered and shook like deranged windup toys, but for every one he and the geist slew, others crawled from under the rotating platform.

Shit. They keep on coming!

"I know everything," the Ringmaster continued. "The only

reason you kept Victor around is to make yourself feel better. Funny how things turn out. This world treated him like the second coming, while you and Beatrice struggled in the slums. But, like always, you put on the 'groovy' facade, trying to hide what you really feel. And for what?"

"Stop! Stop!" Charles clutched his ears, breathing shallow. "I can't!" He coughed, slumping to his knees, shaking. "Ugh!" He tugged his hair, reduced to primal panic.

Only one thing left to try....

Taking a shuddering breath, Victor clenched his fist and punched Charles in the face, just as Dante landed another blow against the Ringmaster's skull.

Shit. Didn't mean to hit him that hard.

"Ow!" Charles stumbled onto his rear. "The *fuck*, man!"

"So! What?!" Victor shouted. "Get ahold of yourself, dude! You feel this way, right?" He looked him dead in the eye. "Well?"

Charles looked up, tears welling, as the Ringmaster quivered with rage.

"Then own it." Victor offered him a hand, mustering a smile. "I'm still your friend. Everyone has a hidden part to them." He looked away. "I know *I* do."

"Then what do you suggest?" Charles spat. "I'm curious."

"Like I said, that's just a part of you." Victor turned to the Ringmaster, who was preoccupied with Dante's defense. "A part of a whole. There's more to you than this. So much more." He cracked a smile. "That's why we're friends, Charles."

Charles looked away, biting his lip.

"Y-you...," he finally spoke up. "Y-you're right. I do feel this way. I mean, deep down. In a very dark place. I'm not gonna lie to you." He wiped the sweat off his brow. "Alright-a." His knees shook as he took Victor's hand. "About time I did this."

215

As Charles walked past the flashing lights, Dante dove on and ahead. The Ringmaster pummeled its fists, its demeanor breaking down into a mad frenzy. It tried to parry the geist's blows to force it back — its fists chipped away, oozing with ichor.

"Yeah, you're a part of me. A fugly one, but *still*." Charles's voice rang past the raging chaos. "I won't give into this trash!" He took a step forward, only for the Ringmaster to ready its fists again, poised to kill. Yet they only slammed against the panels, casting dust and debris in the air as Charles continued down the roulette arena. "N-not gonna work," he stuttered. "It's true, I *am* jealous of him. In many ways. But I'm better than that."

"What did you just say?" the Ringmaster hissed. "You fucking gnat, I'll kill you!"

"Bring it!" Charles shouted. "You're why I'm stuck in this cycle of anger and self-loathing. Wandering without a real purpose. Pretending to be something I'm not. Yeah, you're right about one thing, though. I'm over being second rate." His lips curled into a bitter yet genuine smile. "But I don't need to prove it. Not to you. Especially *you*."

Jesus Christ.

"You think this'll change anything?" The Ringmaster began to panic as Dante hacked and slashed its way forward. "You think this'll make you any better? You'll still be in his fucking shadow! You'll still be the sidekick!" Its voice rose to a metallic scream, staticky and distorted, fading into nothingness. "You'll never be the hero!"

"And I'm surprisingly okay with that," Charles snapped.

"Dante," Victor cried. "Now!"

The geist raised its hand, conjuring twin bolts of cobalt flame, hurling them into the Ringmaster's fists where they caught fire like dry kindling. Then Dante lunged and dove its blade into the daemon's gaping head. Its porcelain cracked

216

like ice under hot water, until the daemon burst into shards of blackness, sending its evil screaming back into the abyss.

And so the other Charles descended, rippling with static as it collapsed on its chest.

"I knew you weren't lying, though." Charles's eyes glistened. "That's the sad part. I just wanted to sweep you under the rug, to make the monsters go away. I was so *ashamed*. But I need to be honest with myself. You see, when the chips are down, *all* this is me."

The specter melded into twilight, a smile on its face, rejoining its master's shadow, bound to Charles's movements once more. A church bell echoed in the distance, and Victor sensed the evil of the Dreadtrain fading, coming to a halt along the railway to madness.

CHAPTER TWENTY-ONE

"Well then," Charles scoffed. "*That* just happened." He ran his fingers through his long, silver hair, turning around. "Victor, thanks for putting up with my shit."

Victor smiled back. "I do what I can."

When the platform descended and the lights faded, there came a song of a different symphony. A band of brass, their taps carrying a jazzy impromptu.

Does he have the same power now?

Charles turned back to his shadow, awestruck, as it metamorphosed again. He reached into his pocket and pulled out a familiar trinket—a pair of emerald dice. And when he held them up, the band was met with drums, keyboards, and an electric guitar. It was the Music of the Spheres, answering to his awakening as a voice spoke.

Dreams have long guided you, Charles. You were an errant soul, wandering from town to town, but you never truly understood what home was. Home is not something you leave behind. It is something that you carry with you. It is something you bestow upon yourself and others, through your true self. Now, let me be free. Let me be a testament to your soul. I am Cesare, the Slumbering Magician.

Dreams have long guided you. Now, it is time that you guide them.
For I am your Anima Firmatis.

And so the geist took form. It was a psychedelic coffin, laden with locks, chains, and tambourine chimes—a wardrobe to wonderland. The doors were marked with masks of comedy and tragedy, opening wide, revealing the magician within. Mummified in a straightjacket, it was shackled by tie-dyed ribbons as its eyes rolled open, swirling with neon light.

It was Charles's soul made manifest, fresh out of a '70s album cover. Then the geist faded back to the Symphonia Mundi, carried away by those fleeting taps.

"What *is* this?" Charles stared at the dice. "My 'true self'? It's like something out of a *damn* funky movie. Hell, it even called itself Cesare, like from *The Cabinet of Dr. Caligari*. Hypnosis and magicians, huh? I can dig."

"A geist." Victor nodded as Dante too vanished. "They're like—Jungian angels. It probably is that same monster, only fettered by your own resolve. The id turned ego." He smiled. "We have the same power, Charles. You've awakened."

Charles's eyes flashed with joy. "That's awesome! But we're pretty much stuck here, aren't we? I don't pretend to know what the hell is going on. This isn't exactly Earth, right?" He gritted his teeth. "I really hate it here, dude. I can't even smoke a good joint. It's all so damn oppressive, you know? And the killer.... This is a *sick* bastard we're dealing with."

"What do you remember from your kidnapping?"

Charles shrugged. "Not much. Just getting chucked in the TV, and this train smacking me dead in the head. You know the rest. Still, with this sweet power, it'll feel nice to not be totally useless. Can't wait to kick some ass."

Victor looked away, remembering the killer's letters. The vitae harvest. The doll-masked daemons and radio surges.

Charles's psychological torture. They were all connected somehow.

"We'll talk about this later," he sighed. "Don't worry. We can find Beatrice and — "

Charles raised an eyebrow. "Then what?"

"Honestly?" Victor shoved his hands in his pockets. "I have no idea."

"Some things never change, do they? Let's get out of here."

"Wait," Victor said. "First off, I have some people I'd like you to meet."

Charles's face turned grim. "The inquisitors? Dude, I remember my time in the riots back in the '60s. That's all I need to know about shit like this."

"If you want to catch the killer, follow me," Victor replied. "They're not that bad, anyway. You'll see. They're fascists, but — they're human about it."

Charles rolled his eyes. "That's *real* comforting."

"Victor," a familiar voice called from beyond the locked entrance. "Victor Roland!"

"Hang on," Victor called, running to the door. He twisted a few valves on the seal, trying to wedge it open like a massive vault. "We're okay!"

With a hiss of steam the door swung open. Thaddeus was pacing back and forth, his metallic footsteps echoing the dimness, as Leng stood by his side, twitchy as usual.

"We heard quite the battle." Thaddeus stepped into the engine room. "And when all went silent, we feared the worst. But enough of that. You must be Charles. Victor has told me everything about you. It is a pleasure to finally meet you."

"I certainly hope not *everything*." Charles tried to smile, looking down. "Nice to meet you too." Then, he pointed at Leng. "Hey. We met back at the Pagoda — I think."

220

Leng grinned. "We did. You were *plastered.*"

"Regardless, I am glad that you are safe," Thaddeus said, a warm glimmer in his eyes.

"Hear, hear." Leng opened his flask, offering Charles a drink. "So, that sounded like a really powerful daemon. And Victor here took it out with Dante, huh? Well done."

"In part." Victor shrugged. "I think it was channeled from Charles's psyche. Just like this place. You said this is his 'sins' made manifest, right?"

"Indeed," Thaddeus replied. "No doubt the daemon went berserk after you denied it. Transforming into a perverse mockery of your darkest thoughts. Am I wrong, Charles?"

Charles laid a hand to his chin. "That does make a lot of sense. But all those hookers died in here too? Like, in their own little slice of Hell? Damn."

"Indeed," Thaddeus said. "As I said, the daemons and Hell are born of human emotion, and tied to our electric power distribution. Whenever the Thirteenth Frequency hits, lesser devils are drawn together and manifest as something far more powerful." He shuddered. "I presume that's how the harlots met their fate. By the hand of their own sins and shadows."

Victor looked away. "And then, they reappear on the telephone poles."

Leng bit his lip, a troubled look on his face.

"However, you have faced yourself, Charles. Which is no small feat." Thaddeus's eyes narrowed. "But judging by what I heard, you also were gifted with a geist. Taming your own shadow into a weapon of righteousness. No doubt your awakening was *not* the Dollmaker's plan. We may have thwarted the culprit, for now."

"Yeah, anyway." Leng turned to the televisions lining the walls. "We used these to get here. Who's to stay we can't use them to get out? As long as they work."

Charles chuckled, shaking his head. "This is *too* weird, man."

With that, Thaddeus raised his electro-staff, channeling its glowing power to the screens. They flickered on as churning portals back to the slums of Holy Gothica. When they stared at the way out, rays of light pierced the Iron Sky. The world felt a little less empty. And as the inquisitors dove into the glass, back to reality, the two friends stood there.

"So," Charles said. "This place is flowing with the Music of the Spheres, huh?" He pulled out his battered Walkman. "That's cool and all, but I got the soundtrack of *my* youth right here." He donned his headphones, pressing that orange button. "Yeah, this is the shit."

"Goddammit." Victor shook his head, laughing. "You're the only person I know who still uses mix-tapes and smokes spliffs. I really did miss you."

Charles patted his back. "Me too, man. Me too."

And yet, for all their fellowship, none would find respite in that city.

CHAPTER TWENTY-TWO

The Thirteenth Frequency had not yet ended. Victor and the others were welcomed by the stench of burning flesh. The horizon was ablaze with chemical fire, screams echoing on the hot, dry wind. And there stood the stormtroopers behind their Kaiser-helmed captain, looming over leprous corpses. No doubt a brutal response to their acts of heresy.

"Something's wrong. This wasn't our protocol." Thaddeus lowered his staff, addressing the squad. "What is the meaning of *this*?"

At that moment the stormtroopers turned their rifles at the four of them. Victor stared down the barrels, sickened with fear—he knew what was happening.

"By order of our Holy Pontiff and Empress," the captain said, "the 105th was dispatched to cull this district. That will be written in tomorrow's paper. As of this morning, Ser Hector Thaddeus and Walter Leng were excommunicated, and will be announced killed in action." She gestured for the squad to take aim. "I promise, your deaths will be clean ones."

"How?!" Leng snapped. "We are her greatest agents!"

"*Were* her greatest agents," the captain replied. "For the

coming reformations, many things must be retried." She stared through Thaddeus. "You are far too dangerous to be kept alive, far too devout to the old ways. A loose cannon—"

"Enough," Thaddeus interrupted. "I have made my choice, and you have made yours. But know that I regret nothing. Can the same be said for you?"

"I have my orders," the captain said, looking away. "It is the Empress's decree."

"The Empress?" Thaddeus stepped forward. "If you are going to betray your commanding officer, at least have the spine to tell me *why*. It is about the Purgatorio Project, no? What happened one year ago, regarding Doctor Murdoch. Expunged from all records."

Hildegarde lowered her pistol, but said nothing.

"I see," Thaddeus continued. "So, she sent you to silence me. Even though my memory was reconditioned to maintain the operation's secrecy. My very existence is enough."

The Purgatorio Project?

"I never claimed to support this action," Hildegarde said. "Even so, I—"

"And that is the difference between us. I am loyal to Holy Gothica herself, not to our figurehead alone. If there is no nation for the likes of me, then shower me with lead."

"No." Victor ran forward as Leng outstretched his arm. "Thaddeus, don't! There's no way you can...." His words dissolved into gibberish, able to utter one word only. "Please."

Thaddeus stopped then, if only for a moment, and glanced back at Victor. And for the first time, they knew their bond was a true one. "I have a last request," he addressed the squad. "Let these two civilians go. They have done nothing wrong."

"I am afraid there can no witnesses. We received specific instructions to purge *all* of you. We cannot allow anyone to know why you were killed."

"Your courtesy has fallen on deaf ears." Thaddeus drew his staff and sword. "The innocents will live." He glanced at Victor with grim pride. "That I promise you."

"You'll not live long enough to keep it." The captain gave the command. "Open fire."

The stormtroopers unleashed a hail of smoke and lead, as Thaddeus and Leng met them with their own steel. Charles tackled Victor aside, and his head cracked against the cobblestones.

He collapsed, dazed, and the raging flames faded to blackness.

#

The reek of smoke hung low. Charles crawled deeper into his haphazard foxhole. Thaddeus and Leng held the line while he dragged Victor behind a battered wall for cover.

"Shit!" Charles spat. "Wake up, man. We have to get out of here!" He tugged at Victor's collar, eyes wide, until he saw a gash across his pale brow. "Dammit."

The fucker passed out on me.

The jackboots closed in—a flamer's blast roared above the rubble. Charles glanced about, looking for an escape. Thaddeus's staff flickered in the darkness as a tesla coil, while Leng dodged and ducked, firing his revolver with wanton vigor.

"There's not enough bullets for this," he shouted, as hollow clicks filled the air.

Then Charles felt something in his pocket, the emerald dice, and remembered that he wasn't alone. Not anymore. He wasn't the same "dirty hippie" as before.

The power to face one's self? The dreams that I guide? Yeah—I can dig.

Thaddeus was about to deal a lethal blow when a riot

trooper jabbed his spine with an electro-rod, and he let loose an agonized cry. Leng bolted to his side until a pair of stormtroopers grabbed him by the arm, throwing him to the concrete with a crack.

I can't just watch. Let's see if it's a power worth using!

The captain was about to give the signal, the troopers' pistols pointed at the inquisitors' skulls, when Charles stood up—knees shaking, bracing himself, counting down as he put on the Walkman. That guardian was fresh in his mind's eye. Straight out of the trips in Burning Man.

Three.... Two.... One....

"Ya'll sons of bitches gonna *die!*" He leapt over the top, screaming, throwing his dice against the smoldering stones. "Cesare, come out to *play-yay!*"

"What is this nonsense?" the captain said. "Do not mock us, you dotard—"

It began like a cyclone of astral imagery—the circles on the dice turned material, cast about on the eldritch wind, overlapping as spheres of neon magic. The stormtroopers doubled back as that totem exploded into swirling smoke. Charles heard the opening riff of his soul and bobbed his head in tune, channeling his other self.

Hildegarde stepped back, giving a shaky gesture. "O-open fire!"

The 105th turned their aim, unleashing a barrage of lead. And yet Charles stood there grinning, as a vortex of tie-dye flame erupted between them, casting the bullets into debris. And from that firestorm, Cesare manifested into reality. The wardrobe swung open, and those spheres launched and exploded like bombshells over the jungles of Vietnam. The Magician Within only cocked its head, unblinking, watching as a purple haze enveloped the stormtroopers.

Hildegarde stepped back, aghast. "W-what the....?"

The stormtroopers shouted in confusion, firing randomly. Charles raised his hand and Cesare charged forth as a soaring coffin of psychedelic doom. Slamming into Hildegarde's chest, the geist's chains wrapped around the troopers' necks, choking and cracking them.

The captain flew against a charred hut, wheezing, staring Cesare in its eyes — they warped and churned, as twin kaleidoscopes. The geist floated ever upward, glowing with altered ecstasy, until those eyes let loose a multicolored blast of energy, engulfing the kill-team in spiraling fractals of destruction. For when it cleared, only broken bodies remained.

The inquisitors staggered up, eyes wide with terrible awe.

"I'm not *the* hero," Charles and Cesare spoke in unison. "But that doesn't mean I can't kick some ass." He grinned as the Thirteenth Frequency ended its broadcast, fading, taking Cesare with it as Holy Gothica's dull, gray reality returned.

"You," Thaddeus gawked. "You have truly awakened."

Charles slouched against the wall, gripped by fatigue. "Yeah, you're welcome."

#

When Victor's eyes rolled open, he felt Charles's hand over his shoulder, and saw the silhouettes of Thaddeus and Leng against dying flames, surrounded by the corpses of the 105th. Beyond the burned shacks there was only silent fog, while the ex-inquisitors bowed their heads, wiping their blades clean. Victor saw Thaddeus's eyes glistening, and not with mechanical pride, he knew.

No, those were tears of shame.

"Why?" Thaddeus choked. "Why us, Leng?"

"Beats me." Leng laid a hand on his shoulder. "We better face it. We're renegades now. Excommunicated. Traitors...."

His eyes lowered to the corpses. "Who just blew up a bunch of stormtroopers. Yeah, there's no going back for us."

Thaddeus clenched his fists. "Then I am truly a martyr, no?"

"That's one way of looking at it."

Thaddeus said nothing, boiling and seething.

"This is getting serious," Charles whispered. "Now what?"

Victor thought this over, carefully. "Well, we still have to find Beatrice. There's nothing for it. We have to—at this rate, who knows what else could happen?" He shuddered, the implications of all this sinking in. "We're on our own now."

Charles gave a somber laugh. "At least you have a plan."

"There is no curse!" Thaddeus let loose a bloodcurdling roar, smashing an iron fist against a wall. "No curse in the tongues of men for such treachery!" He punched and punched, until his knuckles splintered and steamed.

"H-hey," Leng stuttered. "Stop it, Thaddeus. Please. This won't get us anywhere."

"I...." Thaddeus slumped to his knees. "I don't understand, Leng." He gave a despairing chuckle. "Fuck it. Damn it all to Hell."

Victor came to his side, knees shaking. "Thaddeus?"

"Victor." He did not turn to the boy. "You are alive. Good. I am sorry. You should not have to see me like this. I am better than this. I am an agent...." He laid a hand on the dented wall. "No. I am—a good person."

Victor tried to smile. "You pretty much took a bullet for me."

"We all did," Leng said. "Anyway, what's your plan now?"

"I think the better question is, what's yours?"

"Explain," Thaddeus wheezed.

"I'm still going after Beatrice. And the killer is still out there.

I don't know about you, but I doubt the Empress really gives two shits about this. Honestly, I doubt they'll even continue investigating the Dollmaker Murders. If you need a purpose—"

"Purpose?" Thaddeus stood up. "I have no nation to call home, Victor. The Empress is a lying tyrant. In her name, all ties to the Ecclesiarchy were taken from me. I am a *heretic*." His gaze softened. "However, I understand what you mean. I still believe that you are the Far Messiah. If anything, this betrayal has only cemented my faith. Fleeting hope is all I have left. If it is assistance you need, to find your friend, to stop this madman, then I will answer." He knelt on one knee. "I offer you my service, Victor Roland."

"Stop it, Thaddeus." Victor spat. "Get up." The ex-inquisitor paused, but slowly rose, confused. "I don't need a vassal. I need a friend." Victor offered Thaddeus a hand. "I don't want any lords and serfs between me and you. Just the four of us, treating each other like people."

"This unprofessionalism is lost on me." Thaddeus shook his hand. "But I will follow it."

"Then it's settled," Leng sighed. "You three have fun."

"Wait," Thaddeus said. "You're not coming with us?"

Leng raised an eyebrow. "Yeah, no. I'm getting out of this city. Nothing personal, I just can't see anything good coming from this." He looked Victor in the eye. "Anything."

"So, this is it?" Thaddeus's eyes narrowed. "You will abandon everything we've—"

"Say what you want." Leng ran his fingers through his hair. "I really don't care what you think about this anymore, Thaddeus. Sticking around here isn't brave. It's *suicide*. You've seen what we're up against. And we could make it, too, if the Empress hadn't just cut us off from *everything* we've used so far." He looked away. "I'm leaving because I value my life, and I'm not about to waste it on a doomed crusade with a few sleuths."

"Dude," Charles spoke up. "I've said some things that I'm not proud of myself. But that's just cold, man. You'll regret turning your back now. I know I would."

"Let him go," Victor interrupted. "It's fine."

"Thank you." Leng broke a smile, taking a few steps forward. "But Thaddeus is right about one thing. You got brass balls, Victor. I hope to see you again. Someday."

"Likewise." Victor offered Leng a hand. "Thank you, for everything you've done. I understand. And frankly, I don't blame you, but—"

"Yeah, I don't do handshakes." Leng shoved his hands deep into his pockets. "And I'll cut this short with one last inkling of advice. For all of you. Yoshiwara is outside Imperial jurisdiction. It's also the not-so secret headquarters of the Powder Kegs."

"Yeah, what's your point?" Charles asked.

"Think it over," Leng said. "They're a militant insurgency. Who knows, they might actually take pity on a rogue inquisitor and his two acolytes. Anyway, I better get going."

With that, Leng wandered off into the deepening fog.

"There's nothing for us here," Thaddeus said. "As much as it pains me to say, Leng is right. That criminal underworld—it is the best bet for our survival. And the Pagoda awaits us." He turned to the junkyard road. "Lead the way, Victor. This is *your* quest now."

In the shadow of the Train Graveyard, they felt that battle's toll. And as they continued down the rusty way, Victor thought over many things. They had spent so much time confined to Holy Gothica that he'd almost forgotten anything existed beyond. Victor wondered where Beatrice was, and if this rebellion would even accept him. He didn't really know her, but part of him was filled with infatuation for her fleeting memory. In the end, Victor knew it was romanticization—a strange notion, luminous yet hollow. Driven by determination alone, he carried on.

Back to Yoshiwara, to whatever end.

END OF PRELUDE

About the Author

Diagnosed with Asperger's Syndrome at a young age, Fallon O'Neill has been writing since his sophomore year of high school. These scribblings and vignettes would eventually become the earliest drafts of his debut novel, *Geist: Prelude*. Dedicated and passionate, Fallon has worked his novels with the Blue Moon Writer's Group for over seven years, culminating in winning second place at the *Will Albrecht Young Writers Competition* of 2012, and publication in the eighth issue of the *Blue Moon Art And Literary Review*. His favorite pastimes include grabbing a beer (or four) at the local bar, blasting soundtracks into his skull, and watching German movies from the '20s to keep the existential dread at bay.

CPSIA information can be obtained
at www.ICGtesting.com
Printed in the USA
FSHW01n1432031018
52594FS